Belinda Stevens

JUST OUT OF REACH

By Belinda Stevens

DEDICATION:

To my dear friend, Abby Rabinovitz, whose encouragement and suggestions kept me writing when I almost gave up.

Chapter One

JANUARY 17, 1961

There are certain events in life that leave a line of demarcation, the beginning of things, the ending of something else. For me, meeting David was that line.

It all began my freshman year at Lancaster High. What amazed me about the year 1961 was that my feelings for David emerged at the exact moment I became isolated from the soul of my town, my birthplace. I was apart from all that I knew or understood. It all happened so fast that I felt split, like some multiple personality separating into many different identities.

The day we met, it was very cold. The student body had congregated in and around the arcade during morning break to get a glimpse of the falling snow, hoping that the ground would be cold enough for it to stick. Lancaster High was nestled between the canal that separated my town from the residential area and its business district to the north. LHS was made of red brick, with a newly erected concrete arcade leading directly to its front entrance.

As thoughts of a snow holiday raced through my head, Betsy and I noticed a couple at the far end of the arcade. We automatically moved in that direction. I nudged my best friend and whispered, "Who's the guy with Linda?"

"Don't know, let's find out," responded Betsy. My friend continued to talk but I didn't hear a word. My eyes were fixed on the boy at the end of the arcade. My heart was pounding so hard, it was all I heard. My reaction was a mystery, even to me. It still is.

He was taller than most boys his age. Despite his slender frame, the stranger had broad shoulders, but it was his hands and eyes that captivated me. His hands were long and tapered. They denoted a certain strength. His eyes were large and brown. There was a deepness and intensity in those eyes that caught my attention and held it.

Linda motioned Betsy and me over and, with an air of proud ownership, introduced her new boyfriend. His name was David Bhaer.

"Are you any kin to Frederick Bhaer?" I asked.

"Fred's my dad," explained David.

"I can't believe it. You're Fred's youngest son. I mean, I know you have an older brother, Phil," I exclaimed rather breathlessly. "I feel like I know you already. You see, my daddy's Tom Boyd."

"So you must be Katherine," David continued. "Your daddy talks about you all the time. Amazing we've never met."

I gave the excuse that he was a St. Michael's transfer, and I had always gone to public schools. The conversation then changed to the possibility of a snow break and how a few inches of snow closed down everything in central Mississippi. As our conversation progressed, I realized David's eyes never left my gaze. His concentration on me was so complete that I felt every word I spoke was of immense importance to him. I later learned that this was one of David's most charming attributes. His attentiveness would always pull me back. Only death would free me.

Hours later, in the comfort of my overly pink bedroom, I wondered why we hadn't met earlier. Our fathers had been friends since kindergarten. They played golf on Saturdays and tennis on Sundays. Every weekday, Mr. Bhaer closed his jewelry shop around 4:30 and spent the next thirty minutes at Daddy's bank discussing everything from sports to politics. They had maintained the same routine for the past sixteen years. Our mothers were also close. So close, in fact, that Lee Bhaer gave my older sister, Mary Anne, a bridal shower for her first wedding. Not long after I met David, Mary Anne was with her second husband and looking for number three. My sister changed husbands like some women changed moods. With each marriage, Mary Anne hoped to increase her standing in the social register and the value of her bank account.

The more I thought about the situation, the more curious I became. Our families were so entwined that, under normal circumstances, David and I would have grown up together. But my family was anything but normal. Most family gatherings were just that; no outsiders included. Years later, as I watched my Daddy weave his way down the hallway with tears in his eyes and alcohol on his breath, I finally understood. I understood why all social functions required special handling, special circumstances. But on that very cold day in January, I found it strange I had not met David prior to that day in 1961.

Mama was in the kitchen making her special corn casserole when I questioned her about David and the Bhaer connection. The kitchen was my mother's domain and refuge. It was no secret that Mama was an excellent cook who used every pot and pan at her disposal when creating one of her masterpieces, which left the rest of us to clean up the mess afterwards. Most of the time it was worth it, but sometimes I wished Mama was less of a cook and more of a maid. Still, it was amazing the way she could make Baked Alaska without melting the ice cream or burning the meringue. You could enter the kitchen two ways; either from the hallway or the connecting breakfast nook. In the center of Mama's refuge was a wooden island, her favorite working space. On each side of the island were wooden shelves, perfect for storing numerous cookbooks on French, Italian and Southern cooking. On top of the island was Mama's portable radio, which she used to listen to Lawrence Welk and the local news.

As I entered the kitchen, I noticed "the look." It was similar to the look Mama gave me when she told me I was the carbon copy of her mother, Grace. I had my grandmother's large golden eyes, full mouth and fair complexion. According to my sharp-tongued Mama, I also had the same stubborn nature and reckless behavior.

I always seemed to rub Mama the wrong way. My middle sister, Lisa, God bless her, was a saint! Mary Anne was outrageous and full of problems but always in need of Mama's counsel. I, on the other hand, was a constant source of irritation. As I crossed the room, I could tell that she was deep in thought and I had startled her. But there was also fear in her eyes. Mama had a secret she wasn't prepared to share. As she mixed the fried bacon, corn and sour cream, I sat down and propped my elbows on the kitchen table. It was then I asked, "Mama, why don't we ever get together with the Bhaers?"

She answered me with a question. "Why do you wanna know?"

"Because I met David Bhaer today and it seemed odd we hadn't met before," I explained.

Mama's answer was short and edged with anger. "Katherine, how should I know?" she snapped. "Why don't you ask your father? Come to think of it, I would love to hear his explanation."

"But Mama!"

"Katherine," Mama interrupted, "don't you have homework? If you bring home C's this semester, I swear I'll ground you for a month."

It was then that I decided to make myself scarce.

Mama's foul mood lasted through dinner. Promptly at six, Lisa and I entered the breakfast nook next to the family room where the television was located. It's where we had all our meals, except for special occasions like Thanksgiving and Christmas. I quickly realized things weren't going to be pleasant. The frown on Mama's otherwise pretty face said it all. She slammed a large serving dish down so hard on the breakfast table that the sauce from the chicken cacciatore splashed all over the linen tablecloth. This, of course, made her even angrier.

My father, mystified by Mama's behavior, asked, "Pat, what in the world?"

"I'm sick of the TV being on whenever we eat."

"So turn it off. You insist on eating at six o'clock, and I wanted to hear the world news since it's only fifteen minutes long," he explained. "I didn't think you would mind."

"Well, I do. I'm sick of seeing niggers demonstrate. Turning the hose on them is exactly right. If it was me, I would turn those German Shepherds loose, too."

"Pat!" yelled Daddy, trying to stop her tirade.

But this didn't stop Mama. She was good and worked up.

"A few dog bites is just what they deserve."

"Pat, you don't mean that!" said Daddy. His icy tone was a clear warning that enough was enough.

"Maybe not," said Mama, finally noticing the horrified look on Lisa's face. Mama realized she had gone too far.

"All the same, I'm sick of the TV! Tom, turn that damn thing off!" she screeched.

After that, we all ate in silence, afraid to open our mouths for fear it would upset Mama. Lisa and I volunteered to clean up afterwards for fear that Mama, in her present state, would break some of her best serving dishes if left to her own devices.

Later, I heard raised voices coming from my parents' bedroom. I heard Mama say, "Why were you late?"

Daddy, with a sigh, responded, "I told you, Pat, the auditor was at the bank all day."

"Are you sure? Are you sure it's not more of the same?"

"What the hell do you mean?"

"Tom, you know damn well what I mean!" screamed Mama.

At that point, I heard the bedroom door close. Their voices became muffled. It ended the way it always did, with the slamming of doors and my Daddy's car screeching out of the driveway. It would be nearly midnight before I would hear the sound of his Lincoln under the carport. I didn't care, at least not that night. As I drifted into sleep, my last conscious thought was of David and the strange new feelings he evoked in me. While I slept, a blanket of snow covered the ground, giving Lancaster the look of a small New England village.

Chapter Two
JANUARY 18, 1961

I felt bad that I had done it again. I upset the girls and caused a nasty quarrel between Tom and me. I know he isn't seeing Chrissie, but I couldn't forget the past. There was too much water under the bridge to forget.

My husband and children don't know me or my story, except for my darling Lisa. My husband would use my history against me. Of all my daughters, only Lisa listened without judgment and attempted to understand. Mary Anne was too wrapped up in her own problems, and Katherine, close to her Daddy, never really liked me. She would crucify me if she knew what really happened.

It was about a year ago that I told Lisa part of the truth about myself. I was in the kitchen making my special Saturday pancakes, and I was crying. As she entered the room, Lisa heard me and asked, "Mama, what's wrong?"

"Life! Oh, honey, it's a never ending struggle. It's your father and me. We were mismatched from the start." Smiling through my tears, I said, "You girls are the only good thing to come out of my marriage."

"What about the beginning? Was it bad then?" asked Lisa as she took the bacon out of the refrigerator and placed it in the frying pan.

Always Mama's little helper, I thought and answered my daughter with a "yes".

"Sweetie, I'm sorry, but it was wrong from the very beginning. It's as much my fault as your father's," I explained while pouring the blueberries into the pancake batter. "Lisa, I was attracted to your father physically, but the main attraction was the security he gave me."

"You mean because you grew up poor in West Virginia?" she asked.

"No, not really. What I told Tom and you girls is not exactly the truth, or at least not the whole truth," I confessed while pouring the batter into the griddle.

As Lisa set the table for breakfast, I told my middle daughter what I didn't have the nerve to tell the rest of my family. I shared with Lisa things I hadn't spoken of or thought of in years.

"My family was not from West Virginia. My lineage is very similar to your father's. Our ancestors were wealthy landowners from central Kentucky."

"Mama, why did you say you were from West Virginia?"

As I put the finishing touches on our Saturday breakfast, I explained, "Because that privileged existence came to an end when my uncles inherited their father's millions. They managed to drink and gamble their way through granddaddy's money in one generation."

"What about Grandmother Grace? Didn't she inherit any of her father's money?" asked my daughter as she grabbed the nearest chair and sat in it, her curiosity fully evident on her lovely face.

"Yes, but my mother was just as foolish and careless as her brothers. Your grandmother was beautiful and headstrong. She had book knowledge but no common sense, I'm sorry to say."

"So what happened? I mean, what did she do with her inheritance?"

"She married," I said. "My mother was a poor judge of character and rushed headlong towards her own destruction. She married my daddy, who had the looks and the charm but no ambition other than running through someone else's money."

"Didn't anyone try to stop her?" asked Lisa.

"My grandmother saw right through Daddy and tried to stop the marriage, but my mother was hell-bent on having her way and wouldn't listen to anyone. It was an explosive combination; my mother's careless disregard and Daddy's user mentality."

Our conversation was cut short when Tom and Katherine entered the room, ready for breakfast. I leaned over and whispered to Lisa that we would continue our talk later.

As I cleared the breakfast dishes and placed them in the dishwasher, I thought about Mother and how my parents lived high on the hog until the money ran out. After I was born, the funds dried up and Daddy left us. Mother never saw him again, and I grew up without ever knowing the stranger who fathered me.

I went into the bedroom to change my clothes and my thoughts slipped back to those early times with Mother. I pulled a casual dress out of my closet, looked around my well-furnished bedroom and remembered how Mother and I traveled around, living with various relatives. My mother started drinking and partying every night after Daddy left. She would eventually wear out her welcome, and we would look for another relative to take us in. Mother went from man to man. Her looks began to fade and life got much harder.

I sat down on the bed and picked up a picture of my mother, Grace Wells, at the age of twenty and smiled when I thought of Ralph. My step-father was a local miner from the mountains of West Virginia. He wasn't much to look at and poorly educated, but he was kind and he loved my mother. I was only six when he came along, but I felt I had been rescued from the fear I felt, the constant uncertainty of my life with an alcoholic parent. I had just finished putting on my make-up when I heard a soft knock at the door.

"Come in, Lisa," I said.

"Mama, how did you know it was me?" she asked.

I laughed and said, "Your father just walks in without knocking, and Katherine knocks loud enough for the neighbors to hear and, of course, Mary Anne announces herself halfway down the hall."

"You've got us pegged alright," she said, smiling at my observations.

As my middle daughter made herself comfortable, I told her what my life was like in the mountains of West Virginia.

"The basics were scarce," I explained. "I didn't wear shoes in the summer because we couldn't afford more than one pair of shoes for me. I had two dresses, one summer dress and one winter dress, and one thread-bare coat. I didn't know what indoor plumbing was until I left the mountains."

"I can't imagine," said Lisa, amazed at what I was telling her.

I continued my description of life in the mountains. "We lived in a two-room shack. There wasn't any privacy but it wasn't that bad."

"Mama, how can you say that?" my daughter asked. My child who never wanted for anything was trying hard to understand what I was telling her.

"I finally had a home, even if it was a shack, and a sense of normalcy. I knew I wouldn't be moving every couple of months, not knowing what would happen next. Plus, I finally had a father, a good father."

Suddenly, Katherine was knocking on the bedroom door telling me that Perry Mason was on television, a courtroom drama that the entire family watched together. I was glad for the interruption. There were certain secrets, dirty little secrets, that didn't need to be shared with Lisa, at least not now. I didn't tell my middle daughter about Tom's excessive drinking or how I found out about Chrissie.

Hearing Tom's car in the driveway brought me back to the present and the regret over what I had done earlier but then there had been many regrets in my life with Tom.

I was loading the washing machine when the phone rang. It was Frederick Bhaer, one of the few people who knew my story. He was my emotional support, my secret lover, a constant reminder of my private and unyielding guilt. It was mid-day, Tom was at work and the girls were at school. As I picked up the phone, my stomach went into knots; a combination of excited anticipation coupled with my constant companion, fear.

"Hi, baby," he said. "Are you alone?"

"Yes, I'm alone."

"Can you get away?" he asked.

"Not for very long. I can meet you for lunch," I responded.

"Okay. I'll meet you at Angie's."

As I hung up the phone, I realized Fred and I had had that same conversation hundreds upon hundreds of times. Our love affair began in the fall of 1958, but the seeds of that affair started years before when Tom and I were newlyweds.

When Fred asked me why I married Tom, I said, "His good looks, charm, intelligence and old money left me awestruck and breathless. So, after a very short courtship, Tom proposed and I accepted."

"So, it was a spur-of-the-moment thing?" he asked.

"Yes and no. Fred, for someone who had lived in abject poverty growing up, the life Tom offered me was very intoxicating."

But, like I told Fred, it wasn't long before that intoxication was replaced with regret. We didn't even have a church wedding. Tom and I ran off to Alabama and a Justice of the Peace made us legal. On the way to Alabama, Tom told me his parents strongly disapproved of our engagement. Later, I learned that his parent's objections to the marriage made Tom more determined to marry me.

Driving home from my lunch with Fred, I thought about Tom's parents and how much I missed them. To my great surprise and enduring gratitude, Tom's parents became the parents I never had. Their support helped me through some very difficult moments. But that didn't make up for Tom's drinking. It began a few months after we were married, along with the unexplained disappearances. In one of our many rendezvous, I told Fred that Tom's drinking got so bad that his parents considered sending him away to a private hospital. But all that changed when I got pregnant with Mary Anne. After her birth, Lisa and Katherine came in quick succession. When I had my girls, Tom and I settled into an uneasy truce. Unfortunately, the truce was temporarily broken a year after Katherine was born. Tom's drinking got bad again. Later, I learned a chance meeting with the husband of Tom's high school sweetheart triggered the excess drinking.

As I pulled into the driveway, I tried to push out of my mind Tom's drinking binge that almost ended our marriage. At the time, I had no idea what caused Tom's alcoholic binges, but it reached a crisis-point when he went on a ten-day drunk in Birmingham, Alabama. While I was waiting for his return, Tom's parents told me things that helped explain some of Tom's actions and his reason for that behavior. After Tom had been gone for five days, Vincent and Edith Boyd invited me to stay with them until their wayward son returned. I packed a suitcase, grabbed the girls, and hurried to the refuge they offered. Before dinner of my second night with the Boyds, I learned a great deal about my husband.

We were in the sunroom enjoying an early preview of the autumn foliage. As I savored my second glass of homemade lemonade, I learned about my husband's youth, his early problems with alcohol and gambling. But the most startling revelation was the high school sweetheart he almost married. Chrissie, Lee's younger sister, was my husband's first love; the one he had tried to elope with to Alabama. Tom's parents caught them in the act and stopped the elopement. From what Vincent and Edith told me, it was obvious that Tom never forgave them for that.

As we left the sunroom for an early dinner, I realized the real reason why Tom and I ran off to Alabama instead of having a church wedding. I also realized why Tom took so much pleasure in hurting Vincent and Edith. He had never forgiven them for what happened so long ago. It still mattered, and I was about to find out just how much it mattered.

My eyes welled with tears as I thought about what happened when Tom finally returned home. Tom's ten-day drunk in Birmingham led to an awful confrontation between Vincent Boyd and his son. My husband had checked into a motel near the main highway and proceeded to drink himself into a stupor. He returned home around ten o'clock on a Sunday night. Vincent, Edith and I were waiting for him in the playroom.

Vincent, red-faced and furious, screamed, "Where the hell have you been?"

"Birmingham."

"Why did you leave your wife and three small children alone for ten days and go to Birmingham?" demanded Vincent.

"I needed to get away," explained Tom in a low voice.

"And what did you need to get away from? Certainly not work, since you're hardly ever there," commented my irate father-in-law, dripping with sarcasm.

"Vincent, please calm down!" pleaded Edith.

"I am calm, dammit!"

"Dad, I'm sorry, but you don't understand …"

"You're right, I don't understand," interrupted Vincent. "You've got everything anyone could possibly want – a good job, a beautiful wife, and three lovely daughters. But none of that matters, does it, son?"

"Yes, it matters."

"Then stop the drinking and stay home. I had to beg Pat not to leave you, and I wouldn't blame her if she did leave your sorry ass."

"Vincent!"

"I apologize, ladies, but my son needs to grow up and stop disappointing everyone," yelled Vincent, his voice booming, his eyes bulging.

"I'll do better, Dad. I know my girls need me."

"What about Pat?" Vincent asked. "Your wife needs you too, and you'd better remember that!" With nothing more to say, he stormed out of the house, slamming the door behind him.

As I stumbled into the house, my vision blurred by my own tears, I relived the aftermath of Vincent's quarrel with his son. Two weeks after my father-in-law fled our house in a rage, I got a call from Edith. It was five o'clock in the morning so I knew something wasn't right. Instantly awake and dreading what I was about to hear, I asked what was wrong.

Edith, crying into the phone, managed to get out the words, "Vincent – he's dead – heart attack!"

"Oh my God. We'll be right there. Are you still at the hospital?" I asked, throwing off the bedcovers and grabbing for my robe.

Edith and I both felt that Tom's escapade in Birmingham played a role in Vincent's death. My mother-in-law lived another five years before she joined her husband. In those five years, she never confronted Tom, but I'm sure he knew how she felt. Edith was warm toward me but polite and withdrawn around her middle son. I guess I didn't help either. I made it pretty clear through my sarcasm and periodic outbursts what I thought of the situation. Despite the passing of time, Vincent's death still caused me pain.

Grieving over the loss of Vincent wasn't the only difficulty I had to cope with. Shortly after Tom returned from Birmingham, I discovered I was pregnant again. Not sure that the marriage would last, I decided to abort. The procedure took place in Dr. Pierce's office. Everything was stark white and the room felt cold as ice. Dr. Pierce was very gentle with me.

"Pat, it will only take a few minutes. You will feel a pull on your stomach but it shouldn't hurt," he said, patting my hand in an attempt to reassure me.

It took only twenty minutes, but it seemed much longer. I

felt the pull and it did hurt. But worse than that was the sucking sound. I will never forget that sound! After it was over, I cried for days. I promised myself I would never go through that ordeal again, no matter what happened to my marriage. I never forgot my unborn child. Thinking of Vincent and Edith brought it all back with a vengeance. As I entered the kitchen, I reached for the phone and called Fred to make plans for the next day. I needed him to drive away the memories.

I was numb from the news. As I listened to Dr. Pierce, my mind seemed to separate from my body. It was like my family doctor, the same doctor that had delivered my girls, was talking to someone else. I thought I had been so careful but, obviously, not careful enough. I was pregnant, and Tom was not the father! I thought about my last pregnancy. This time I knew I would not abort. Other than that, I didn't know what I was going to do. As I drove home, I thought about the events that had lead to my present state; all the things Tom did wrong and the things I did wrong as well.

After Birmingham, things settled down somewhat. For the girls' sake, Tom stopped drinking. But we still fought over everything from civil rights to how I raised the girls, especially Katherine. She was her father's favorite, and Tom felt she could do no wrong. My youngest daughter was very independent and had a strong, stubborn streak in her. No matter how I tried to force her to behave, she fought back. It always led to tantrums, tears, and eventually spankings. As my daughter grew older, the fighting between me and Katherine worsened, with Tom acting as a referee. The fact that my husband sided with Katherine enraged me. This, of course, widened the gulf between me and Tom. We were like strangers living under the same roof, barely speaking to one another. There were days and sometime weeks of silence between the two of us. Things rocked along unchanged until the fall of 1958.

It all came to an abrupt halt at the Bhaer cookout which was in honor of Lee's birthday. Tom and I didn't socialize with other couples due to Tom's drinking, but the cookout was an exception. It was my best friend's special day and I wasn't going to miss that.

Unfortunately, my husband was having a secret affair with his high school sweetheart, which had heated up. He had gone from seeing Chrissie once a month to four nights a week. I knew something was up. What I didn't know was my life was about to change dramatically. Torn between his love for Chrissie and what he was doing to his family, Tom started drinking again. He began to sneak a drink or two which usually led to three or four. By the afternoon of the barbeque, he was three sheets to the wind. Later, Tom told me he had considered divorce and moving away from Lancaster with Chrissie, but leaving the girls was something he couldn't think about, at least not sober. Tom and I took separate cars. He arrived around two o'clock and weaved his way through a few guests who showed up early. Tom spoke to Frederick, who was busy marinating the chicken, shrimp and steaks for the cookout. Chrissie was decorating the backyard and patio. After speaking to his friend, my husband made a beeline for Chrissie.

I arrived around three o'clock and noticed my husband talking to Lee's younger sister, the one Vincent and Edith had told me about. I watched as my husband, with his arm around Chrissie's waist, steered her toward the house. It was four o'clock, all the guests had arrived, and the backyard was pretty crowded. No one seemed to notice as Tom and Chrissie entered the back door. And no one seemed to notice that I had followed them. As I made my way down the hall toward the master bedroom, I could hear them. In between the loud kisses, I heard Tom say, "Chrissie, I love you. I need you, baby."

"Not here, Tom."

"I can't wait -- please, baby."

There was more kissing and then silence. Suddenly, I heard laughter and then the mattress began to creak. I opened the door and saw the startled looks on their faces. Chrissie was topless, and Tom's pants and underwear were down around his knees. Chrissie's legs were wrapped around her lover's waist. I cried out. I'm sure my face registered the array of emotions I was feeling

-- shock, disgust and acute sadness. As I turned to run away from the humiliation I was feeling, I ran straight into the arms of Frederick. He later told me he had decided to take a bathroom break and had made it halfway down the hall when he stumbled into the ugly scene that was unfolding. Fred had the presence of mind to pull me from the room, slam the bedroom door, and guide me down the hall to another room. Fred held me until I calmed down. He found a handkerchief in a chest-of-drawers near the middle of the room and gave it to me to dry my eyes. He asked, "Are you okay? I mean, of course you are not okay, but is there anything I can do?"

"I'm fine," I interrupted. "Actually, I'm not really surprised. I knew something was going on; all those late nights."

"What do you mean late nights?" he asked.

"For a long time now, Tom's been leaving after supper and not returning until well after midnight," I explained, my face hot and flushed red with anger. "At first it happened once or twice a month but, lately, Tom's been staying out late at least three or four nights a week."

Obviously shaken and saddened by my explanation, Fred responded, "Pat, I'm so sorry. I knew Chrissie had separated from Martin, but I had no idea."

"How could you?" I asked.

"I can assure you that Lee knew nothing and certainly wouldn't condone this and neither do I."

"I know, I know. What I don't know is what am I going to do now?" I said, walking over to the mirror to survey the damage, as I put it.

As I powdered my nose, Fred helped me develop a temporary game plan. Neither of us would tell Lee or anyone else what had happened. I would confront Tom later that night and Frederick insisted that I meet him for lunch the following day.

Tom was waiting for me when I got home. He was so drunk he could barely stand up, but that didn't affect his ability to express himself. I asked him why.

"You want to know why?" he screamed.

"Yes, why?" I screamed back.

"Because I love her! I've always loved her. Something I don't feel for you," he said.

His words felt like knives slashing at my chest and stomach area. He could see me wince, but that didn't stop him.

"You know I only married you to get revenge on my parents. I never loved you." He spit out the words like some obscenity. I tried to stay calm and asked in a steady voice.

"How long have you been seeing her?"

As he moved across the den and poured himself another bourbon and water, Tom turned toward me and said, "Almost from the beginning of our marriage."

I felt like someone had punched me hard. It took my breath away. I asked, "Then why did you stay with me all these years?"

"For my girls," he responded. "You haven't been much of a wife --certainly not a proper companion. Your only saving grace is the fact you bore me three daughters. Thank God my genes are in the girls. I can only hope that their blood isn't polluted by you and your hillbilly relatives!"

With that, my horror and sadness turned to rage. In an instant, I hated him!

Suddenly, Tom stood up, swaying from side to side, and said more, "Chrissie and I used to laugh at how inept you were. You have no class, and you never will. Just like the poor white trash you are, you constantly harp on civil rights to make yourself feel more important…"

I interrupted his tirade with a scream, "Get out of here, you bastard. I never want to lay eyes on your again!"

With that, he stormed from the room, grabbed a suitcase, and slammed the back door. As I heard his car screech out of the driveway, as it had so many times before, I dissolved into tears.

Tom went to the local motel -- the only one in town. I met Fred the next day at Angie's around eleven o'clock in order to beat the lunch crowd. I barely touched my sandwich. I guess I looked pretty awful and certainly drained considering look of concern registered on Fred's face. With tired, bloodshot eyes, I told Frederick what had happened the night before.

"Tom said he didn't love me and had never really loved me." With that, I cast my eyes toward my plate, too embarrassed to look Fred in the face.

He took both of my hands in his and said, "Pat, you don't deserve this, and I know you want to leave Tom, but don't do anything yet. A lot of things are said in the heat of the moment, and then there are the girls …"

In a voice dull and flat, I continued, "Fred, you can't imagine how nasty he was. He said every under-handed, below-the-belt thing he could think of. I don't know if I could stand to be in the same room with him after this."

"I'm sorry," said Fred. "It's your life. I shouldn't have said anything. Just know I'm here for you."

"I know, and I'm not going to do anything yet," I assured him. "I need to let the shock wear off and then I'll decide." I took a sip of my sweet tea and continued.

"Tom said he loved Chrissie. He's staying at the Lancaster Motel. I told him to get out! Fred, it's not just what he said to me, it was the way he said it. His words were so vicious. His voice was filled with so much pent-up anger."

"Was he drunk?" asked Fred.

"Yes, but it was more than that." I explained. "It was obvious that my husband -- the man I thought I knew -- could barely stand being near me."

Fred, shaking his head, said, "I've known him all my life, my best friend, and I don't understand his actions. Pat, let me talk to him before you do anything. Please, for the sake of the girls …"

"Okay, okay," I interrupted. "I'll wait, Fred."

As we were leaving the restaurant, Fred hugged me and said, "Let's meet back here day after tomorrow. That will give me enough time to talk to both Chrissie and Tom."

"Do you think it's necessary to talk to both of them?" I asked.

"Yes, Chrissie is my sister-in-law. I believe she will be expecting to hear from me after what happened at the barbeque."

"Okay, Fred, whatever you say," I said in a tired voice.

"Pat, I'm here for you. We'll get through this together, I promise."

His words comforted me. I smiled at him. It was the first time I had smiled in days.

Several days later, I met Fred again for a late afternoon coffee and a piece of Angie's famous apple pie. When I saw Fred's smiling face, it was the first time in two days that I relaxed. I felt the tension leave my body as Fred put his arms around me and gave me a quick hug.

"How have you been holding up?" he asked. As I looked into his eyes and answered him, I felt his kindness, his compassion, for me.

"It's been kind of tense with the girls. They don't understand why their Daddy isn't home. I made up some excuse, but I think they realize something's up," I explained. "How did your meeting with Chrissie and Tom go?" I asked, not sure I wanted to know the answer.

"Chrissie didn't need much convincing that she was in deep trouble. She told me she didn't want to lose Martin; that Tom was more or less a fling that never should have happened – a trip down memory lane, she called it."

"Well, she can have him for all I care!" I exclaimed.

"Let me finish," cautioned Fred.

"Chrissie, also, begged me not to tell her sister. She said she was going to have it out with Tom last night."

"What about Tom? What did he have to say for himself?" I asked, dripping with sarcasm.

"He didn't have a chance to say a lot," laughed Fred. "I read him the riot act. I told him the minute I sat down that I had met with Chrissie and that I hoped I had talked some sense into her. I also told him that Chrissie had agreed with me as to my assessment of the situation."

"Really -- and, what did Tom say to that?"

"His exact words were 'Fred, I don't want any interference from you.'"

"That sounds like him," I said while sipping my coffee.

"Well, that's when I blew up and called him a selfish bastard. I told Tom that if he didn't end the affair, I would never forgive him. I shouted so loud that I think I scared the waitress."

"And what did Tom say?"

"He pointed out that we had been friends since grammar school. He couldn't believe what I said."

"He probably couldn't. He isn't used to people standing up to him. At least not since his father died," I interjected.

"I pretty much told him off," said Frederick with a rueful smile on his face. "I told him I didn't care how long we had been friends. Again, I said, 'if you leave Pat and the girls for Chrissie, you can kiss our friendship good-bye.' I told him I meant it."

"Did he believe you?" I asked, polishing off the last of my apple pie.

"He said he didn't understand, so I made it perfectly clear for him. I told him everyone close to him – everyone who's ever cared about him – was sick of his selfish, mean-spirited ways. I told him that he never thought of anyone but himself. Then I said that I would help him patch things up with you, but I would be damned if I would stand by and watch my friend destroy his family. With that, I stood up, threw a few dollars on the table, and left as quickly as I had come."

When Fred had finished, I put both my hands on his and said, "Fred, you can't imagine how much I appreciate everything you've done. Your friendship and support means everything to me, but I just don't know. I don't know if I want to patch things up."

When I got home, Tom was waiting for me. I couldn't help myself. All the anger and disappointment came to the surface when I said, "Well, look what the cats drug in."

"I guess I deserve that," said Tom rather meekly.

"You deserve that and a lot more," I shot back.

"Please, Pat, let me talk," he pleaded.

"Why should I listen to you? I've had enough of your insults, your put-downs. Maybe I don't have your pedigree, and maybe I'm an insecure bigot, as you put it, but I'm not a vicious drunk who puts his family at risk by having sex with his high school girlfriend," I screamed.

"Do you want the girls to hear you?" he asked.

"No," I said. With that, we went into the bedroom and

closed the door.

"Again, Tom, what are you doing here?"

"I want another chance."

"That's not what you wanted several days ago. What changed your mind, other than sobering up?"

"I had a long talk with Fred and Chrissie."

"I know about Fred," I interjected. "When did you see Chrissie?"

"Several hours after Fred told me off. I met her for dinner ..."

"Oh, how cozy!"

"Please, Pat, let me finish. Chrissie made it clear that it was over between us. She didn't want to lose Martin."

"So you came crawling back because you didn't have anywhere else to go. Is that it, Tom?" I said, raising my voice again.

"No, that's not it. I mulled over everything that's happened recently, and Fred's words cut pretty deep."

"And, what, pray-tell, did you conclude from all that mulling over?" I asked, hating the very sight of the man standing in front of me. I wanted to slap him, but I resisted the impulse.

"That it is time to grow up. Pat, I know I've been a selfish prick and I don't blame you if you never forgive me. But, if you give me another chance, I promise things will be different. I love the girls, and I want to be there for them. I want to be a good husband to you and a good father to the girls. Please, Pat!" he begged.

Suddenly sad, I responded, "Tom, I don't know. Too much has happened. I don't know if I can forgive and forget."

"Pat, I understand. But, for the girl's sake, let's try."

He held out his arms and came towards me. I pushed past him, turned, and said, "Okay, but here are the ground rules: no more drinking, no more sex, and that includes me. Until I decide otherwise, I'm off limits to you."

I then left the room to let my husband mull over the ground rules. Tom agreed to my terms, but the tension between us was evident for everyone to see. We didn't fool anybody, not even the girls.

We remained friends with the Bhaers, but there were no more attempts to socialize with them or anyone else as a couple. I continued to see Fred with Tom's encouragement. Tom knew Fred was acting as a go-between, a counselor.

Sometimes Tom would join us, but would leave early so I could vent to Fred. Both knew I couldn't talk to Lee, so Fred was the next best thing.

We would meet for lunch once a week. At first, our lunches were an exercise in vitriol against my husband. But, as time passed, I began to look forward to our luncheons with anticipation. Because of my past, I've always been insecure and suffered from acute shyness. I tried to cover it up with a false reserve. I surprised myself by opening up to Fred. He was so sweet and so obviously interested in what I had to say. I couldn't help but tell him my secrets. I shared with Fred my painful past and how I couldn't forget the hurt Tom had inflicted upon me. The words my husband spoke the day I caught him with Chrissie continued to haunt me. As much as I tried, I couldn't let go of the rage I felt towards Tom. As our luncheons continued, my relationship with Fred evolved from friend and confidante into something more complex and intimate. Fred also shared private thoughts with me, such as his strong connection with his family.

I'll never forget the day he told me about Lee. We were eating sandwiches at our favorite haunt, Angie's, when I asked, "How and when did you meet Lee?" I said as I swallowed the last morsel of my turkey club.

"Unlike her sister, Lee didn't go to school in Lancaster."

I smiled and said, "Tell me more."

"She went to Sacred Heart in Vicksburg," he responded.

"Why did she do that?"

"At one time, my wife considered entering a convent."

"You're kidding," I said, totally surprised by Fred's revelation. "She never told me."

"Well, anyway, that's why I didn't know her until after the war, or at least until after my service in the Army. You know I received an early release due to my injury that left me with a limp. At least I got the use of both legs," he laughed.

As he continued, his eyes lit up when he talked about Lee. "She went to work in my daddy's jewelry store, which I eventually took over."

"So, like me, you met your spouse at work, with a lot better results," I said, half joking.

Ignoring my comment, Fred continued, "Daddy hired Lee to help prospective brides pick out their silver and fine china and to list them on our bridal register. I couldn't take my eyes off of her," said Fred, smiling as he relived the memory of that first meeting. "She was almost as tall as me, as you know -- a beautiful brunette and those deep-set eyes. She took my breath away!"

"I'm envious."

"I'm very lucky. Lee's wonderful and my boys … what can I say? They're everything to me."

"I understand," I said, patting his arm. "My girls are everything to me."

"Tom said you fight about Katherine?" questioned Fred as he pulled out his wallet to pay the bill.

"Yes, she's strong-willed -- just like her grandmother. I don't want my daughter to end up like my mother, Grace."

It was then I told Fred my darkest secret; the one I later shared with Lisa. His reaction was a combination of horror and rage. He told me how he wished someone had been there for me. He also said he would be that someone from now on. I pointed out to Fred that he had a family to take care of and that I wasn't his responsibility. His reaction caught me off guard.

"I know, Pat. I know where my responsibility lies but that doesn't mean I can't be your friend. You never had a brother. Well, I'll be that brother for you. Is that okay?" he asked.

"Yes," I said, so grateful to have Fred in my corner.

As I got into my car, Fred leaned over and patted my arm and said, "Remember, I'm here for you, my brave little friend."

I smiled at him and said good-bye. As I drove off, I thought -- yes, sometimes brave, but sometimes very fragile. Suddenly, I felt frightened. Everything felt so raw. My thoughts were chaotic and I couldn't make sense of them.

Spring came early that next year, and Fred and I decided to take advantage of the fact. We took a ride in the country after lunch. I was telling Fred how I had tried to self-educate myself into someone Tom could be proud of. I had just finished explaining how my husband didn't appreciate the French cooking or my attempts at high fashion, when my friend took me in his arms and kissed me. Suddenly, I pulled away and mumbled under my breath, "Please stop."

Fred apologized over and over again. "Fred, it's okay," I said. "Please understand, Tom's a real jerk, but Lee's my friend. Plus, we can't hurt our families."

"I know, Pat. I'm really sorry."

"And, it's really okay. I cherish our friendship and these last six months have been great. You've been a real life saver for me. But, I think we shouldn't see each other again, at least not alone. I don't want to tempt fate."

"You're right, but remember if you need me, just call."

Our resolve lasted a month. I couldn't stop thinking about Fred. When he called and asked me to meet him in Jackson, I readily agreed. He told Lee he had to meet with a man about an estate sale. Among the estate items were several pieces of antique jewelry that Fred said he wanted to look at. I told Tom I was going to spend the afternoon shopping for shoes. That's when the lying started, followed by the cheating. We got ourselves a room at the Robert E. Lee and made love, for the first of many times. I felt awkward and shy but Fred was so gentle. He pulled me toward the bed, stroked my hair, and kissed my face. I quickly relaxed in his arms. Afterwards, we snuggled and talked.

I alternated between intense longing for Fred and overwhelming guilt. I knew he was going through the same thing. He felt as conflicted as I was. He told me if it was possible to love two women at the same time, then he did. I felt horrible. Lee was my best friend, but I needed Fred. The attention and comfort he gave me helped to ease the years of verbal abuse I had suffered from Tom.

We tried to break off the affair so many times I couldn't count. Each time we failed miserably. Fred couldn't stop thinking about how devastated Lee would be if she found out, not to mention his sons. What would Phil and David think if they knew the truth? And then there was Tom, his best friend, who thought Fred was helping keep his marriage together when, in fact, Fred was making love to Tom's wife. It got to the point he couldn't sleep and had the beginnings of an ulcer.

My state of mind wasn't much better. I hated Tom, but I loved my girls, and I loved Lee. The guilt was eating me up. I couldn't sleep. There were nights I ended up pacing the floor until dawn. If I had been a smoker, I would have gone through a pack a night. As it was, I almost wore a hole in the rug from pacing back and forth. Everyone noted my moodiness, as well as my volatile and unpredictable nature, and my family suffered for it. What had once irritated me now enraged me, and I couldn't help myself.

Finally, when I couldn't stand it any longer, I called Fred and asked him to meet me at a Jackson restaurant, NOT the Robert E. Lee. We met at Primo's. I took a few bites of my gumbo and blurted out, "Fred, it's got to end -- this thing between us! I can't take it anymore. The guilt is consuming me, and I'm taking it out on my family."

"I know, I know," he said. "You're right. I can't bear it either. The guilt is eating me alive, literally," Fred exclaimed, pointing to his stomach.

"Honey, this time we have to stick to the plan. We can't give in. Too many people will be hurt -- destroyed. You know that, don't you?" I asked.

"Yes, I know, but I'll always love you, Pat, and I'll always be there for you." I could hear the sadness and resignation in his voice and see it in his eyes.

With that, we kissed and parted, but not soon enough. Two weeks later, Dr. Pierce told me I was pregnant -- again! I was still numb with the news when I called Fred. He had taken half a day off from work to play golf with Tom. He was walking out the back door when the telephone rang. He told me later he almost didn't answer it. Fred grabbed the phone in the den and answered with a gruff hello.

"Did I call at a bad time?" I mumbled, my voice so low Fred almost couldn't hear me.

"Kind of -- I was just leaving the house to go play golf with Tom."

"I'm sorry, Fred. I wouldn't have called if it wasn't important."

"I'm sorry, too. I didn't mean to be rude," he responded, obviously sensing that something was wrong, very wrong.

"I don't know how to say this except to blurt it out. I'm pregnant, and you're the father."

After a short silence, Fred said, "I know I'm the father. You didn't have to say that."

"I apologize, Fred. I just didn't want you to think there was anyone else, certainly not Tom."

"You don't have to say anything. We're in this together," he assured me. "I need to sit down and catch my breath," he explained. "I don't have the energy or enthusiasm left for golf, not now."

I urged Fred not to cancel his game, and I then told him, "Dr. Pierce says I'm about eight weeks, so I have to do something fast," I said, the panic evident in my voice.

"We'll get married. I'll talk to Lee today!"

"No!" I screamed. "I won't let you hurt her! If we do what you suggest, too many people will be hurt; your boys, my girls, and our unborn baby," I reasoned, calming down as I spoke. I already knew what had to be done.

Fred interrupted my thoughts with a question. "Then what's the answer? What can we do?" he questioned.

"Let's meet at Angie's tomorrow, and then we'll decide. Let me think this through," I responded.

"Okay," agreed Fred.

"I didn't call you for a quick answer," I explained. "I just felt you needed to know."

After I hung up, I quickly put my plan into action. I arranged for the girls to be out that night. I cooked my husband's favorite dinner and plied him with several gin and tonics. The results were just what I expected. The next day I had lunch with Fred. As I slid into my chair and picked up the menu, I told my friend, my lover, my confidante, "I'm going to pass the baby off as Tom's."

"That means you'll have to sleep with Tom."

"I already have," I confessed.

As shock and disgust registered on Fred's face, I continued, "Fred, I'm going to sleep with him again to make this lie more plausible."

"The thought of you sleeping with Tom and passing our baby off as his makes me sick."

The look on his face said it all, but it couldn't be helped and I told him so.

"It's too late for either of us to take the high road; we must do whatever is necessary to protect the innocent ones. We will have to live with the disgust and shame. That's our penitence, Fred, for what we've done."

"I know. I can't argue with that, but it doesn't mean I have to like it."

Fred and I were never alone together after that last luncheon at Angie's. We kept in touch through sporadic telephone calls and letters that Fred wrote to me. I received the first of those letters several days after our last meeting.

My darling – my little friend with the sad eyes:

> *I miss you and I'm sickened with what you were forced to do. I know to do otherwise would hurt too many people.*
>
> *Please remember I love you. My greatest regret is that I can never acknowledge our baby. It hurts more than words can describe.*
>
> *If you need me, remember I'm a phone call away.*

Love, Fred

I was able to give Fred a parting gift that he was always grateful for, and he told me so numerous times. I insisted that Lee and Fred be Godparents to our baby.

Chapter Five
DECEMBER 8, 1962

Dinner started easy enough but turned into a verbal battleground between Mama and me, with Daddy acting as referee. Daddy wasn't very successful, but he did stop Mama just short of a slap across my face. Sometimes, when he wasn't around, the slaps came hard and fast. Many times I wanted to crawl in a hole or scream until someone rescued me. Other times, I wanted to stomp Mama into the ground.

The fight began when Daddy mentioned Fred Bhaer's afternoon visit. "Fred says Phil's wedding is about to drive him crazy; that his house has been turned upside down due to out of town guests and the rehearsal dinner tomorrow night."

"I can't wait," I interjected.

"She's suffering from puppy love," snickered Mama.

"It's not puppy love," I shot back, embarrassed that Mama would bring it up at the dinner table.

"Who's my baby in love with?" asked Daddy.

"David Bhaer, of course, who else does Miss Priss constantly talk about, other than that nigger preacher?"

Mama's remarks made Daddy uncomfortable. "Pat, let's not go there tonight," Daddy pleaded.

Although Mama was not from Mississippi, she quickly took up the more negative aspects of being a Mississippi native. In an attempt to fit in, Mama embraced the racial attitudes and blatant ignorance of those around her. It was one of the many subjects my parents violently disagreed about. Mama's attitude fit like a glove with her basic insecurities and the dark fears that seemed to consume her.

Sometimes my mother would appear to be mildly irritated by my father's differing views. Other times, his beliefs, as well as mine, seemed to enrage her.

Mama's loud, sharp voice brought me back to the present as she slammed her hand on the table and said, "Tom, you better take your daughter in hand. If anyone knew how she felt, God only knows what would happen."

"You act as if I'm not here," I interrupted.

"I know you're here, and I don't want any more of your nigger-loving talk in this house or anywhere else. Do you understand?" screamed Mama.

"You can't tell me what to think, what to feel!" I screamed back.Quick as a flash, Daddy caught Mama's hand in mid-air as I ran from the table in tears.

It reminded me of last September. We fought then, Mama and me. It was the night Ole Miss rioted and federal marshals came to Oxford. I watched events unfold that entire week: the threats of secession by Ross Barnett and Governor Wallace of Alabama; the refusals to enroll James Meredith, a Negro, at the University of Mississippi; and the Saturday night football game with the giant rebel flag, the band playing Dixie as Governor Barnett promising the cheering crowds that Ole Miss would never be integrated. It reminded me of Nazi rallies, the ones I had seen in old news reels.

By Sunday, the inevitable happened. The news that Meredith had secretly registered and was hidden away in one of the dormitories spread across the campus. Students began to gather, shouting obscenities and threats. Things turned ugly in an instant; tear gas, bricks hurdling in the air and cars turned upside down and burning. There were news bulletins on television. And I, along with my family, gathered around the TV set, everyone except Mama. She claimed she had better things to do. Daddy said life was going to change and Mama couldn't stop it by acting like an ostrich. Mama went into the kitchen, refusing to acknowledge any of it, until President Kennedy appeared on TV, pleading for calm. Mama rushed from the kitchen, shouting, "The stupid son-of-a-bitch doesn't even know about the rioting he caused."

As usual, I disagreed, "If anyone caused this mess, it's Barnett. He's the one who stirred everybody up. It's his fault, not President Kennedy's."

"Katherine, you're a damn fool. Someday, someone's going to kill that son-of-a-bitch and I can't wait," screamed Mama, her lovely face contorted into a vicious snarl.

"I hate you," I screamed back.

Daddy wasn't fast enough. Mama slapped me, leaving a red mark on my right cheek. Later, I turned the faucet in the bathroom sink to full force, so Mama couldn't hear me crying. My tears were a mixture of anger and fear.

My thoughts quickly returned to the present as my sister entered my bedroom.

"Don't let Mama get to you," advised Lisa. "She's under a lot of strain right now and has a lot to deal with."

"What's she upset about now?" I asked.

"She's pregnant, Katherine, and not really sure what to do. Dr. Pierce wants Mama to abort because of her age."

"She can't do that," I said.

"She's done it before," explained Lisa.

"When and why in God's name?" I asked.

"It was a year after you were born, and she and Daddy were going through rough times."

"Mama and Daddy are always going through rough times," I interrupted. "I still can't believe she did it. Did Daddy know?" I asked.

"No, and you can't tell him, not ever! Look, I know it's hard. Mama's not easy, but you don't know what she went through growing up. It was awful," explained Lisa.

The look on my sister's face clearly indicated that she knew more than she was willing to tell. That was Lisa, the perfect confidante who you could trust totally, knowing she would never reveal the secrets you shared with her. It made me wonder what my mother had shared with my sister that she didn't share with the rest of us.

"That still doesn't explain why she digs at me about Kennedy and King. She knows how I feel about them," I said.

"That's just it. She's afraid others will know. Mama's afraid it would affect Daddy financially. His bank is a small bank in a small town. What would happen if he lost local business?"

At that moment, I couldn't help feeling Lisa was too forgiving, too willing to make excuses for Mama.

Later that night, much later, I thought about the little sister or brother I would never know, and if my mother ever thought about that lost child, the one she threw away.

DECEMBER 10, 1962

Trinity Episcopal Church was the oldest standing church in Lancaster. In fact, it was the oldest in the Diocese. The Church was erected in the 1820's, not long after Mississippi became a state. A gothic structure made of old brick, its inner sanctum was wrapped in lush red carpeting, ornate stained-glass windows and prayer benches made of dark mahogany. Trinity was a beautiful church, increasingly so at that time of year, and precisely on that particular day. Phil Bhaer, David's brother, and his bride-to-be were going to be married at Trinity that night at eight o'clock.

I remember the church was decorated in holiday colors of red and green. Red poinsettias, green ferns and holly adorned the altar, while red candles gave off a warm glow that lit up the church. I also remember how I felt that day. I could barely contain my excitement. In a few hours, I would see David at his brother's wedding. I had thought of little else for the past two weeks. Since I had met David on that cold day in January, he had crowded my thoughts. I longed to take Linda's place. When they broke up in mid-November, I was elated. And now, Phil's wedding would give me a chance to get David's attention, to whet his appetite, so to speak.

I took extra care in getting ready that night. As I looked in the mirror, I realized the white wool suit, set off by my red raspberry shoes, had that "Jackie look." It was a look I wanted to cultivate, and Mama helped. If Mama said a certain suit or dress looked like Jackie, then I would insist upon wearing or buying that particular article of clothing. It seemed ironic to me that Mama hated J.F.K. and yet wanted me to dress like Jackie. However, that very inconsistency was somehow consistent with Mama's personality. Style and good taste were important, an obvious reflection on the marketability of goods, meaning me and my value on the marriage market. Mama was hoping I would eventually attract the right sort of buyer with a no return policy.

When Mama and I went shopping, she was like a different person. Full of fun, Mama laughed a lot and displayed a well-developed sense of humor. Her eyes seemed to light up her face. But it never lasted. Brief glimpses into that other side of her made me wonder who was the real woman -- this happy, laughing lady, or the other one, the woman who slashed out at me and left a red mark on the side of my face.

As I entered the green-carpeted hallway that led to the kitchen, living room and front door, I was amazed at how lovely and young my mama looked that night. She wore royal blue, a color that emphasized her black hair and fair complexion. I wondered how such a tiny woman could create such fear in all of us whenever she willed it. Daddy was prematurely gray, but he seemed years younger than Mama. His blue eyes held none of the sadness that dominated Mama's face. Sometimes, I would catch Mama in a whispered telephone conversation. When she noticed me watching her, Mama would abruptly hang up and ask why I was listening in on someone else's conversation. I often wondered if those secret phone calls had something to do with her incessant sadness.

Mama never seemed young although she wasn't old. It was hard to believe that our President, who seemed decades younger, was actually the same age as my mother. Daddy, on the other hand, reminded me of Peter Pan. That contrast between her oldness and his perpetual youth accented the difference between the two and aggravated the clashes between them.

As we left for the church, my excitement and nervousness grew. The butterflies in my stomach fluttered furiously. By 7:45, Trinity Episcopal Church was packed with friends and family of the bridal couple. I glanced over my shoulder to watch David escort his mother down the aisle. Lee Bhaer was dressed in a winter green flowing gown that was fitted at the waist. The design accented her tall willowy figure. It was obvious that David had inherited his looks from his mother, who had the same deep-set eyes and brown hair. My heart began to hammer as he noticed me and winked in recognition.

Phil Bhaer's bride looked lovely in her mother's dress. The shoulder length lace veil fell softly over her face, and the fitted satin bodice of her wedding gown advantageously accented her full figure. As the couple spoke their vows in Trinity Church, my thoughts were filled with David. Suddenly, I felt I would always love him and that somehow, someday, we would be together. I think the day I met David, those feelings took seed and began to grow. By the night of the wedding, they consumed me. Sometimes I was frightened by the strength of my feelings. It didn't seem natural.

After the wedding, my family made a brief appearance at the Lancaster Country Club to wish the couple luck before heading home to television and a late snack. The country club was set on a hill overlooking the town. At its center was the clubhouse which included a pro-shop and a reception hall where the after- wedding festivities were held. The hall was filled with people weaving around and between cloth-covered tables laden with a four-tier wedding cake, assorted mints and nuts, finger sandwiches and a punch bowl filled with crushed ice, ginger-ale and seven-up. There was also a champagne fountain for those who wanted something stronger than punch and a large center-piece comprised of magnolias.

I waded through an army of people and a receiving line to get to David. He was surrounded by a group of admiring females, each with the same goal as mine, to get his attention. When David saw me, he waved me over and told me how pretty I looked. I returned the compliment by saying, "So do you," which made him laugh. We talked briefly about his brother Phil, football and the fact that David had made the team. At that point, Daddy announced it was time to leave. As I left the reception hall, I glanced back at David and caught his stare.

During the short ride home, I euphorically interrupted my parents' conversation by announcing, "Someday, I'm going to marry David Bhaer." Both stopped mid-sentence and turned with incredulous stares toward me. There was also fear in Mama's eyes.

Chapter Six
JANUARY 8, 1963

I was glad to be home again. Lisa and I had spent most of our Christmas vacation with my sister, Mary Anne, at her apartment in New Orleans. She had recently separated from husband number two. Mama said, "Mary Anne needs the comfort and company of family," so she shipped us to Louisiana. Neither of us wanted to go. I was hoping to hear from David, and I knew Lisa didn't want to leave Ray Harridge. Ray and Lisa had been dating for three years. It was an open secret that they would get married after college. He had won a scholarship to Vanderbilt, and my sister was going to Ole Miss. They were going to spend every vacation and holiday together.

Most people thought they made an unusual couple. But I understood the attraction. My sister would speak to strangers, while Ray shied away from people and buried his head in books. He confessed to Lisa that his childhood years had been very lonely. Ray was the only kid in his neighborhood. His sole playmate was his dog, Millie, a black and white Border Collie that followed Ray everywhere. He would spend after-school hours exploring the woods near his home with his furry companion.

Ray was what people would call a nerd; a dedicated bookworm who was both non-athletic and uncoordinated. He felt isolated on the playground; always the last one picked for red-rover, and no one wanted Ray on their softball team. He laughed when he told Lisa that he invariably ended up in the backfield, never catching the occasional fly ball.

When he told Lisa about his childhood, she said that he was so smart and, according to her, that meant a lot. Ray told me he understood what Lisa was saying. Yes, his science projects always won first place at the annual Science Fair; he could figure out every mathematical problem, even the obscure ones, but as he pointed out to me, that didn't win him any friends. According to Ray, the popular boys were outgoing and good at games, and Ray wasn't either of those things.

Ray told me that things didn't get any better as he got older, they got worse. His shyness seemed to grow. Until Lisa came into his life, he barely nodded when spoken to. In the classroom he was a star, the teacher's pet, but when the bell rang everything changed. Ray said he would close his books and shut down verbally and emotionally. He told me he would have made himself invisible if that had been possible. As he went from class to class, Ray would bend over his books, trying to make himself less noticeable while brushing against the walls, always staying in the shadows.

When he told Lisa what he had told me, she leaned toward Ray, kissed him and told him there was no need to hide in the shadows anymore. He told me her words meant a lot to him.

That was a year ago. Lisa was a cheerleader and class officer. She brought Ray into her sphere and he, indeed, was no longer in the shadows.

Ray was completely devoted to my sister. His eyes would follow her even in a crowded room. They walked hand in hand to class and when Lisa spoke, Ray listened. To Lisa that was everything. And that's what made Lisa and Ray a good match.

I wouldn't say Ray was good looking in a conventional sort of way. As a matter of fact, he was tall and gangly. His large eyes were hidden behind oversized glasses. He had a full head of brown hair that no comb could tame. I guess it was his innate sweetness that made him appear handsome.

Ray and Lisa were a study in contrasts. Where Ray was tall and uncoordinated, Lisa was petite and graceful. Unlike Mama in temperament, my sister did inherit Mama's physical attributes. She had her dark hair and eyes, as well as her pale complexion. She also had Mama's curves and, like my mother, Lisa was a stunning beauty - the kind of beauty that made people stop and stare. Whenever I mentioned that fact, she would make a joke out of it and change the subject.

My sister and Ray hooked up during first semester of their sophomore year. Biology was Lisa's least favorite subject. She laughed and said it was ironic that she met the love of her life in a class she literally hated. Ray later told me that he had a crush on Lisa for almost a year before they met.

Everything changed the day he first noticed her. Almost a foot shorter than he, a tiny little thing, to him she seemed larger than life. Love at first sight didn't begin to describe how Ray felt when Lisa looked in his direction that early fall day of his freshman year. By the time they finally met, he knew almost everything about her family background, her friends, and even her after-school hobbies. As it was said in The Godfather, Ray had been struck by lightning. Long after they began dating, his parents labeled his feelings for my sister as a schoolboy crush. But he knew better. He couldn't believe his luck when Mr. Robinson assigned Lisa as Ray's lab partner.

He said Lisa took his breath away the moment she entered the class with her fast-gaited walk and a grin that lit up her entire face. Ray said she spoke to everyone in the room. He loved the way she made the unpopular, the shy and the unattractive feel important, special. According to Ray, there was nothing fake or self-promoting in her actions. She really cared. I agreed with him.

As my sister sat down beside Ray, her grin widened.

"Hi, I'm Lisa Boyd."

"I know," he replied.

"Guess you're stuck with me for the semester. I have to confess, I'm lousy at Biology. And the thought of cutting into a frog makes me queasy."

"Don't worry, I'll get you through it," said Ray, trying to reassure his lab partner.

Lisa smiled again and said, "I know you will. Now tell me about you. What's your story?"

Ray said he talked more that first day than he ever had before. He said she was so easy to talk to. It was though he had always known her. He told Lisa how he wanted to go to a really good college and become an engineer. His dream was to work for NASA. After class, my sister invited Ray to the Circle, a local drive-in situated at the end of the main drag, next to Center and Ridgeway Roads. It was little more than a whitewashed one-story wooden building located on a gravel parking lot but a major gathering place for teenagers. A car-hop took their order and came back with a tray of food and attached it to the window of Lisa's car. Ray said they laughed and talked and ate homemade fries until it was time to go home. He felt blessed just being Lisa's friend; he couldn't imagine ever being anything else.

Afraid he would never get up the nerve to ask her for a date, she made the first move and asked Ray out, a fact that he couldn't believe. It was beyond Ray's imagination that anyone as beautiful and sweet as Lisa would want to go out with him. At least that's what he told me. They went to see some beach party movie, watched Sandra Dee attempting to surf, and held hands the entire time. Later, they parked near the levee and spent most of the night talking. Again, it was Lisa who made the first move. She leaned over and kissed Ray in the middle of his lecture on black holes in space.

After that, they were an item, something that surprised everyone, at least at first. As time passed, those that mattered accepted Ray and began to see what Lisa saw in him -- a really sweet guy who truly loved my sister. Gradually, they both changed. Thanks to Lisa, Ray was more at ease, more willing to speak up around others. And Ray had his affect as well. Lisa's grades improved. My sister became an avid reader. Her thinking was less dependent on certain preconceived notions. She started to question our parents' views and challenged her teachers on a wide range of issues. Ray said it pleased him to watch her grow mentally and to know that he played some small part in that growth. They seemed so calm, so relaxed with one another. Their happiness was obvious. But Lisa was neither calm nor happy about the trip to New Orleans.

Our bedrooms were connected by a common bathroom, so I could hear her sobbing. I entered her room and knelt beside the four-poster bed. The varying shades of blue and green that decorated Lisa's bedroom mirrored her normally serene personality.

"What's wrong?" I asked.

"It's our senior year and my last Christmas before college. And with Ray going to Vanderbilt and me to Ole Miss - well, we've made a lot of plans and now I have to break them."

"I'm sorry, really sorry," I said. "I don't want to go either."

"Because of David?" she asked.

"Yes, I told Mama and Daddy I was going to marry him some day. Now, I wonder if that's wishful thinking."

She wiped her eyes and smiled.

"I think if that's what you want, it will happen. It's up to you, sweetie."

I smiled back. I had come to comfort Lisa, but I was the one who was comforted. But that's how it was with Lisa and me. Even when we were little, she would make things better. She was the ultimate big sister, taking care of me and defending me against everyone from the school yard bully to an angry Mama.

As I fell asleep that night, I thought about all the plans Lisa and Ray had made for their future and not just the immediate ones. My sister wanted a small family wedding. Ray wanted a honeymoon in Florida, close to NASA, of course.

They even talked about the number of children they would have and when to start their family. A year after Ray was accepted as an engineer and Lisa had found a suitable place to live, they would start their family. Four children sounded right. It didn't matter to either if they were girls or boys as long as they were healthy and happy.

I wondered if David and I would ever be as close as Lisa and Ray. So close, in fact, that they finished each other's sentences and thought the same thoughts at the same time. I felt bad for them, that they had to be separated even for a short period of time. I understood Lisa's reluctance to leave Lancaster. I wondered why Mary Anne's divorce was allowed to interfere with everyone's plans, mine included. I turned red in the face just thinking about it.

Despite our misgivings, part of the trip was fun. Mary Anne was a pain in the ass, but New Orleans was an exotic adventure for two teenage girls. The three of us spent our mornings drinking coffee and devouring beignets at the Café du Monde in Jackson Square. We lunched at the Court of Two Sisters, dined at Galatoire's and savored egg custard in the opulence of Antoine's.

Lisa and I took a carriage ride through the Quarter and I had my fortune told by a gypsy woman in the Square. We spent a full day in Audubon Park, and the next day Mary Anne took us to shop at Maison Blanche and D.H. Holmes. She even arranged for us to attend a floor show at the famous Blue Room. I loved the old-world atmosphere of New Orleans and the way it came alive at night with crowded streets and music blaring on every street corner.

But there were other sights and sounds that were not so pleasant, such as Negro men shining shoes that were carelessly referred to as "boy," and signs that separated the races. Even public water fountains in the park were labeled "Whites Only" and "Colored." It reminded me of a book I had read the previous year, <u>Black Like Me</u>. It was the story of a white journalist who temporarily darkened his skin and traveled throughout the Deep South as a Negro. As I walked down Canal Street, I remembered what the author said about New Orleans. Public restrooms were nonexistent for Negroes, and sometimes he had to walk miles with a full bladder. As I rode through the Quarter in a horse-drawn carriage and sipped my coffee at the Café du Monde, I wondered about those shoeshine boys and day laborers. I wondered if they had trained themselves to hold it. Or maybe they just went without food or drink until they were safely in their own neighborhoods. That book had a way of invading my thoughts. As I looked at those tired, dark-skinned faces, I suddenly felt uncomfortable in my own skin.

There was another factor that lessened my enjoyment of New Orleans, namely Mary Anne. At times I could laugh at my sister's remarks. This wasn't one of those times. I wanted to gag Mary Anne with a washcloth, scarf, or anything handy, as long as it muffled the sound of her voice. It started the day we arrived. First came the incessant whining about husband number two.

"Thank God you're here. You can't imagine what I've been through with Richard's lawyer. He has no soul," wailed Mary Anne in a high-pitched voice.

"Would it be possible to unpack before we get into your legal battles?" I asked, straining to carry my suitcase and hanging bag up the staircase. Mary Anne's dining room, kitchen, and den were on the first floor, her three bedrooms on the second floor. I didn't like Mary Ann's apartment. It was too modern for my taste, all glass and chrome. The atmosphere of the place seemed to clash with the old-world feel of New Orleans. Everything was white. Her living room sofa and chairs were white. Even the carpeting throughout the apartment was off-white. To make matters worse, the canopy of Mary Anne's bed was covered in white mosquito netting, not to mention the white satin bedspread that engulfed her king-sized bed. The living room walls were decorated with black and white photographs of Paris, the only thing in my sister's apartment that appealed to me. There were also family pictures placed in all the bedrooms. Most of the pictures were of Mary Anne. After we got settled in the menagerie of white, my sister's tirade continued.

"I told that jerk I needed at least four thousand a month to maintain myself."

"You've got to be kidding!" I said, barely believing what I was hearing. Forty-eight thousand dollars a year was a fortune in 1963.

"Why should I be kidding?"

"Because that's a lot of money, Mary Anne."

"It's necessary if I'm going to entertain and be part of society," exclaimed my sister.

"And why is that necessary?"

Ignoring my question, Mary Anne continued. "I can't believe Richard is being so difficult after all I went through," screeched my sister, her pitch rising with each word.

"Lower your volume-you're hurting my ears," I said. "And just what did you go through?" I asked.

Mary Anne's second husband was a descendant of one of the founding families of Memphis. Richard's father and grandfather had vast land holdings in west Tennessee and both had been on the Board of Directors for the Union Planters' Bank. For that reason, my sister thought her married life would be full of shopping, travel, and non-stop socializing with what she referred to as "the upper crust." Richard proved to be too studious and too settled for Mary Anne. She took to calling him "spacey Richard' or the "foggy-minded professor." Eventually, their conflicting lifestyles led to a parting of the ways. When I asked my sister what she had put up with, I knew I would get a long-winded and often repeated answer.

"How would you like to be constantly ignored and never go anywhere? I was literally stuck in that dinky little house in Memphis."

"Five thousand square feet isn't dinky," I responded.

Ignoring me, Mary Anne continued. "My life was unbearable. You just can't imagine. Lisa, dear, I hope you think long and hard before you marry that four-eyed Ray. You don't want to end up like me," she snapped.

Mary Anne's success with men had taken on legendary proportions by her twentieth birthday. She was an outstanding beauty, with long legs, auburn hair and large green eyes. My sister was thoroughly skilled in the art of charming and snaring men with seemingly little effort. Her first marriage before her eighteenth birthday was to a wealthy Delta farmer who was six years her senior. This union lasted barely six months. Mary Anne's never-ending ridicule of his long sideburns, red-neck behavior and lack of breeding finally took its toll. Mama had been against the marriage but Daddy for some reason said Mary Anne was old enough to know her own mind. Within a year, she remarried to Richard. By the time Mary Anne was twenty, her second marriage had run its course.

My sister's harangue continued into the second day of our trip. It was a beautiful and surprisingly warm day for January, so we decided to have our breakfast in the courtyard. Unlike her apartment, Mary Anne's patio reflected the lush, exotic ambience of southern Louisiana. It was made of old brick and overlooked a garden which could only be described as a profusion of indigenous flowers and exotic plants, including every color in the rainbow. There were several banana plants, numerous gardenia bushes, wild roses, azaleas, purple irises and a group of dogtooth violets. In the center of the courtyard was a wrought-iron table and chairs with plush red cushions in each chair. The table was covered with trays of food - - croissants, fresh fruit, muffins, scrambled eggs and sausage -- that was served on Mary Anne's fine china. All of this was hidden away from the busy traffic of the French Quarter by old brick and heavy foliage and securely enclosed within a wide wrought-iron gate. While she drank breakfast tea, her slender fingers carefully curled around her demitasse, Mary Anne began her attack.

"Lisa, explain to me why you're dating Ray Harridge. I mean, he's not cute. He has no money and no family to speak of. So why him?"

"I love him," answered Lisa.

Ignoring the answer to her question, Mary Anne continued."Look, I know you're limited in your choices, but not that limited."

Sick of her mouth, I counter-attacked. "Look who's talking about choices. You're about to get a second divorce and you're not even twenty-one."

"Katherine, this isn't necessary," said Lisa with a tired voice.

"Oh, yes it is. Mary Anne's full of opinions and advice. Well, it's time she got some advice in return," I yelled, feeling downright smug.

"Katherine, I don't understand why you're acting this way. I love you. You're my baby sister," drawled Mary Anne, exaggerating and emphasizing every word. It sounded more like a threat than an expression of affection. I could almost feel the knife slowly churning in my back.

"I just want to know why you're such an expert," I continued. "Why are you passing judgment on Ray? Remember Deke the redneck, with dead animals on his wall?"

"Deke was a Delta farmer," interjected Mary Anne.

"He was a dumb redneck with mutton chops," I shot back.

At that point, Lisa defused the situation by reminding us we needed to get dressed if we were going to hit the shops before the traffic picked up.

As we tried on clothes, mainly skirt and sweater sets and a few newly arrived spring formals, it started again. "Lisa, you're fat!" exclaimed Mary Anne, as though it was a newly discovered secret. "Is that a size ten?" she asked.

"No, it's an eight," responded Lisa.

"Well, it's too tight. You need a ten. While you're here, it wouldn't hurt to make an appointment with my hairdresser. Your bangs are too long. You look like a sheepdog."

"Why do you always have to be such a bitch?" I asked.

Mary Anne gave me a hurt look and started with the fake tears. Lisa got upset, pulled me aside, and asked, "Why can't you leave it alone?"

"For the same reason you won't defend yourself. It isn't in my nature," I said.

"For my sake, will you please drop it!" she pleaded.

"Okay," I said.

"And apologize!" demanded Lisa.

"Okay, okay. Look, Mary Anne, I'm sorry. I didn't mean it."

My sister smiled a thin-lipped smile and triumphantly accepted my begrudging apology. After that things calmed down until the day before we left. Little did I know that Mary Anne's latest crisis would give me the opportunity I needed to connect with David. Mary Anne could be both a source of amusement and irritation. I was amazed that anyone would wrap empty packages to put under a Christmas tree, just for the sake of appearances. But how things appeared was part of the program aimed at promoting my sister's social status. Even her cat had to maintain its high standing in the animal kingdom. Precious, however, failed miserably. Six weeks before we arrived, she gave birth to a litter of kittens that were part blue-point Siamese and part alley-cat. The father of this "less than pure" breed was Kit-T, the neighbor's gray tom. There were five in the litter. Mary Anne had managed to find homes for four. I suggested that she keep the last of the litter, but Mary Anne would have none of it.

"Why should I want the mongrel offspring of that mangy tom? If I had my way, he would be at the vet's right now!"

"I'm sure your neighbor would love that, not to mention Kit-T," I joked.

Mary Anne was not amused. Lisa and I ended up taking the kitten home with us. As luck would have it, David's aunt agreed to take the last of the litter. David volunteered to pick up the kitten and deliver it to his aunt's house. He was scheduled to come by two days after we got back from New Orleans. I was excited and a little bit nervous. It would be the first time I had seen David since his brother's wedding.

Chapter Eight
JANUARY 12, 1963

I waited on the sundeck for David. The deck overlooked the two streets that intersected and formed the corner of Magee and Stonewall. My heart skipped a beat when I saw David's car come around that corner. I picked up the gray and white kitten and opened the iron gate that led to the sundeck. As he entered the deck, David leaned over and kissed me on the cheek.

"Hi, Katie, how was New Orleans?"

"Great, but I'm glad to be home."

"Why's that?"

"A little dose of Mary Anne goes a long way," I said.

David laughed and took the kitten from me.

"Katie, would you like to go to the diner for Cokes and fries?"

"Sure," I said, happy and nervous at the same time. After delivering the kitten to David's Aunt Jewel, we turned onto Savannah Boulevard and drove to the Blue Bird Diner.

When we arrived at the diner, David took my hand and led me to a booth in the corner. He punched several buttons on the juke box and Fats Domino's "Walkin' to New Orleans" filled the room. The diner was a collection of red leather booths with a jukebox in the rear. The floor of the diner was covered in black and white tile. A counter near the front entrance provided special treats. You could watch a soda jerk serve up homemade lemonade, cherry Cokes, or the best butterscotch sundae east of the Mississippi.

I looked into David's eyes and suddenly my face flushed red. My tongue felt four inches thick and my brain went numb. Thankfully, David took the lead.

"Katie Boyd, what do you want to be when you grow up?"

"I don't know. I guess I'll get married and have a family," I responded, my face still red.

"Is that it?" questioned David, his eyes searching for answers.

"No, that's not all, but I'm a little embarrassed. I've never told anyone."

"It's okay, I won't repeat what you say."

"I want to go to Washington to be a Kennedy aide, or at least meet the President someday. I want to shake his hand." I shook as I repeated the words.

"He's not my hero, but if that's what you want, then do it."

"What do you want?" I asked

"To be a pilot."

"Really?"

"Yeah, since I was eight."

"What happened when you were eight?"

"Mr. Niven took me up in his private plane." Mr. Niven was a local crop- duster who gave free rides to local kids on the weekends. "I need to fly like you need to breathe."

"I know what you mean," I responded, "and to play tag with the clouds."

"That's right, how do you know that?"

"My Uncle Jack," I explained.

Jack was Daddy's younger brother and my favorite uncle. He was two years younger than Daddy and very outgoing. Tom Boyd had two older brothers but it was Jack that everyone doted on, including my grandparents. He was a wonderful athlete and a straight-A student. Jack learned to fly during his junior year at University of Tennessee. He had planned to attend law school at the University of Virginia, but after his first solo in the air, Uncle Jack knew he wanted to spend the rest of his life flying planes. My grandparents were not thrilled with his decision but learned to accept it eventually. During the war, he flew missions over Germany. In the late forties and fifties, Jack belonged to an elite group of test pilots who flew the hottest new planes over the desert of California. He was there when Chuck Yeager broke the sound barrier in 1947. He knew them all - Scott Crossfield, Jim

Lovett, Wally Schirra. I loved it when Jack came for a visit and told me stories about the war and his adventures in the California desert. I shared all this with David.

"Uncle Jack says flying is the closest thing to God on this earth - like you could almost touch His face with the tips of your wings."

"Your uncle sounds like quite a pilot. Is he still flying?" asked David, brushing a strand of hair from my face with his slender fingers.

"Only for fun," I replied, my voice cracking with nervousness. "He's married now and works for McDonnell-Douglas."

The next day, I got a telephone call from David asking me to a dance in Leflore County. It was held at the Greenwood Elks Club, forty miles north of Lancaster. I spent two hours getting ready. Lisa, of course, helped me pick out my dress and participated in the make-up and hair process. Mama, on the other hand, seemed less than excited over the prospect of me and David. Sometimes when she didn't know I was looking, I would notice a fearful, teary-eyed look on her face. Whenever I mentioned David, Mama would almost wince. I didn't understand it since Mama and Daddy were such good friends with David's parents.

As Lisa was helping me roll my hair, I mentioned my concern to her.

"Lisa, Mama seems less than enthusiastic over David and me."

Lisa laughed and reassured me, as she pulled another strand of hair over a roller and snapped it into place. "It's your imagination, Katie. Why in the world would Mama object?"

"I don't know, but I get the feeling she does."

"Baby, that doesn't make sense."

"Since when does Mama make sense?" I answered back.

When the doorbell rang, my heart jumped at the sound. I saw David standing in the living room door and wanted to run into his arms, but everyone was watching. I simply said "hello". As we walked to the car, he took my hand in his and said, "You look fantastic."

I thought to myself, so do you! I couldn't take my eyes off him; his shoulders, his eyes, and the smell of him. While we were dancing, I buried my face in his neck and breathed in the scent of him.

I think there are moments, and they are few, when you feel everything is so right, so special, that you want that moment to go on and on. You never want it to end. That's how I felt that night. I wanted our date to go on forever. I was as happy as I would ever be. I couldn't imagine it getting any better than that night at the Elks Club.

That was the beginning of our time together. After that, we went to Friday night basketball games, the picture show, and dances at the school gym. We held hands, necked in the front seat of his car, and talked endlessly about anything and everything.

I would meet David after football practice. He had an old black car that looked like something out of the 1940s. We would ride around in that old wreck that he loved, or go to the Circle and talk. Boy, would we talk! The months that followed were idyllic for me. I shared my private thoughts, my most secret feelings. I told David how I felt separate and apart from my neighbors, even friends. Unlike most of Lancaster, I was disturbed by the burning bus in Anniston, Alabama, and disgusted when thugs smeared ketchup on the heads and faces of young demonstrators at the Woolworth's lunch counter in Jackson. I shared all this with David and how witnessing history both frightened and excited me.

I'm not sure David agreed or even understood what I was saying. But he listened and appeared interested in everything I said. I reveled in his attention and blossomed under his studied focus.

I asked him how he could listen to me for hours and hours. "Don't you ever get bored with me?" I asked one afternoon when we had just circled the main drag for the tenth time that day.

He gave me a quick smile and said, "Katie, you may be a lot of things, but one thing you're not is boring. I'm getting quite an education listening to your afternoon rants," he laughed.

"Thanks a lot." The hurt in my voice was pretty obvious.

"Baby, I'm sorry. I didn't mean to offend you."

"You sounded like you were making fun of me," I said, refusing to look at David, somewhat angry with him at that moment.

"Katie, I wasn't making fun of you. I wish I had your passion, your commitment. I'm somewhat in awe of you."

"Thank you, David," I said, instantly forgiving him.

I looked deep in those brown eyes of his and wondered if he had any idea how important he was to me. I had been criticized for my outspokenness. David was the first person to encourage my openness, my willingness to say exactly what I was thinking.

My world took on a brightness and beauty I had never known. That year, spring seemed to be resplendent with newly discovered sights and sounds. The fragrant scents and colors of dogwood trees, red, pink and white azalea bushes, sounds of sparrows singing, crickets chirping, the clean smell of fresh rains and the whirl and tumble of March winds seemed deliciously new to me.

One day in particular stood out in my memory and symbolized what that spring was like. It was a Saturday and David surprised me with a ride in the surrounding countryside and a late afternoon picnic. We found the perfect site, a meadow filled with wildflowers, the scent of which assaulted my senses. There was a small creek several yards away shaded by river birch. After stuffing ourselves with fried chicken and pound cake, we swam in the creek. As we were laughing and splashing one another, David pulled me close and kissed me.

"Do you know how much I love you?" he asked.

"I think so," I responded. After a long pause, I said, "I feel the same way."

He kissed me again. I wanted to freeze that moment and make it last forever.

Sometimes we would take his motorcycle out on a dirt road

near a cotton field and ride for hours. I loved the feel of the wind in my hair and on my face. But more than that, I loved my arms around David's middle and the feel of my chest against his back.

David was always surprising me with small thoughtful gifts that represented the many things we shared that spring and early summer. However, none of that prepared me for what happened on my birthday. I really thought he had forgotten it, and I wasn't going to remind him. On the day in question, we decided to go to the diner for fries and a Coke.

As I opened the door to the diner, everyone screamed "Surprise!" There stood my family and all of my friends from school. The diner was covered in white and blue balloons and streamers. In the middle of the room was a birthday cake surrounded by numerous presents. David had arranged the whole thing. What I loved most about that very special birthday was David's gift. It was a gold heart-shaped locket with his picture inside. He also gave me perfume and flowers, but it was the locket that made the greater impression on me.

Later that night, we kissed until my lips were bruised, and I felt dizzy with my need of him. My longing was so intense, I felt like I was about to be swallowed into an abyss and disappear forever, where nothing of me was left except this overwhelming desire to wrap myself around him and become part of him. Sometimes I would wake myself from a deep sleep calling out his name. Sometimes Lisa would hear me in the next room.

I loved to watch David with others and the way he related to each individual whether they were young or old. With my young cousins, he was patient and involved. David would spend hours dragging toys out of their playpen and entertaining them with whatever he had in his hands -- a truck, a ball or a stuffed animal. He was respectful and attentive with his elders. He never seemed bored or distracted. He gave his full attention to whoever was speaking and showed interest in whatever he or she was saying. It amazed me how David could listen to my father tell the same stories over and over again. Even I got bored with some of Daddy's often-repeated tales. But David didn't care. He genuinely liked my father and enjoyed his company. When I think back on that very special spring, I can't help but smile. At the time, I treasured each moment I had with him. Despite this, I was fearful that none of it was real. I would wake up one day and realize I had imagined all of it.

Chapter Nine
MAY 14, 1963

Late spring brought new and interesting changes in my family, and David was still by my side. The twins were born on May fourteenth. They were delivered by C-section and didn't have that freshly pruned look that most newborns possess. They were named Quentin and Daniel. Each was distinctly himself and equally lovable to me. Quentin did push-ups in his bassinet, while Daniel lay there playing with his fingers, gurgling, and giggling interchangeably. I could tell early on that both would be fair-haired and that their blue eyes would probably remain blue.

Mary Anne came home to be with Mama the week prior to the twins' birth. Daddy called it "the gathering," the circling of the wagons, so to speak. Despite his jocular mood, Daddy, along with the rest of us, was very anxious over the birth of the twins. The last few weeks had been hard for Mama, and she took to wandering the hall of our home at odd hours. This led to a caravan of family followers, with me bringing up the rear. Mama, in exasperation, ordered each and every one of us to our respective rooms. Daddy, however, proved to be resistant, exclaiming, "Please don't leave me at a time like this!"

Later everyone would laugh about Daddy's response, but at the time it was no laughing matter. There was Mama's age and the fact she was carrying twins.

Once the ordeal was over and Mama and the babies proved to be fine, everyone relaxed and enjoyed the arrival of Quentin and Daniel. Mary Anne was particularly excited, but not entirely due to the birth of her little brothers. It seemed my sister had a new boyfriend. It appeared she had fallen in love for the first and only time.

Mary Anne was single again and very much in the market for a suitable mate. Her first encounter with Terry was something she enjoyed relating to all who would listen. My sister viewed life as a breathless interval, from one great moment to the next. She was waiting, always waiting, for another moonlit scene, the next Prince Charming who was predestined to complete her incomplete self, the individual who would not only provide her with all the material comforts but would also make her completely and sublimely happy.

With a heightened sense of drama, Mary Anne related how she was dining with friends at Corinne Dunbar's when the couple first eyed each other and continued to glance in each other's direction throughout the evening. When the red-headed stranger left the dining room, Mary Anne followed. She watched him pay his bill and open the door to his red Porsche. As Terry pulled away from the curve, Mary Anne jotted down the numbers of his license plate. The next morning, she contacted a friend at the local courthouse who secured the mystery man's name, address and telephone number. My sister then contacted the local florist and ordered a single yellow rose to be delivered to Terry's address. In less than twenty-four hours, she received Terry's reply, a dozen red roses and an invitation to dinner. After that, they were a couple.

Terry's father had made a fortune by providing school supplies and athletic equipment to numerous school districts throughout the South. Terrance Hessler was his father's southeastern regional manager, with all the skill and finesse of a super salesman. I couldn't help but wonder if life wasn't one big sales pitch for Terry. I wasn't the only one who felt uncomfortable around him. Lisa was also concerned. One night in early June, she expressed those concerns to me.

"I have this vague feeling, an uneasiness."

"I know, so do I," I said

"Katherine, I never felt that way about Richard or Deke, but Terry, I can't explain it. I don't like it."

"Neither do I."

"I wish I could talk to Mary Anne, but we've never been able to talk. I regret that."

"It's because she's jealous of you," I explained.

Lisa laughed. "Why in the world would Mary Anne be jealous of me?"

"Because you are loved by everyone. You're so sweet, so understanding."

"No, I'm not, but thank you anyway."

"Well I'm glad you're around," I said, hugging my sister. "It's nice when your sister's also your friend."

With laughter in her eyes, Lisa hugged me back. She was especially happy that night. She and Ray had gone to a dance at the community center in Belzoni. She wore a green sundress and gold loop earrings that matched the charm bracelet Ray had given her for her birthday.

"Katie, it was one of those soft summer nights in the Delta filled with the sounds of crickets rubbing their legs together. The air itself smelled like freshly cut flowers."

"A perfect summer night."

"Yes, perfect. We slow-danced to all my favorite songs. Ray said he would always remember my arms around his neck and the smell of me on his clothes."

"You're kidding. That doesn't sound like Ray."

"I know. You should have heard us on the ride home," she laughed. "We both sounded like love-struck teenagers."

"Well, that's what you are," I said.

"The drive home was magical. He put his arms around me and pulled me close to him. I rested my head on his shoulder and looked up at the sky. Katie, it was clear and so full of stars. At that moment, Ray asked me what I was thinking about. Naturally, I said I was thinking how perfect the night was."

"And?" I asked.

"I told him I was thinking of all the perfect nights ahead of us and the life we would have together, not to mention our babies," she laughed.

"And what did Ray say?"

"He said he hoped they would be beautiful like their mother," said Lisa, blushing from the neck up. "I told him I hoped our babies would be smart like their daddy."

"Your looks and Ray's smarts -- you can't beat that!" I said, hoping that David and I would end up like my sister and the boy she loved.

That night we both fell asleep with smiles on our faces.

JUNE 12, 1963

June 12 would be a date I would never forget. There were several reasons for this. Forth-five miles south of Lancaster, a lone sniper shot Medgar Evers in the back and left him to die in the driveway of his west Jackson home. I was watching Johnny Carson when the local station interrupted programming with the news. I thought of President Kennedy's speech earlier that evening and how he talked of the need for civil rights legislation. I wondered when the bloodletting would end. Little did I know it was just beginning!

It must have been three in the morning when the phone rang. But it was Mama's screams that woke me. It sounded like someone was ripping her flesh. I ran into the hallway and saw Daddy holding Mama up. She was shaking uncontrollably.

"Daddy, what's wrong?" I asked. My stomach felt like a block of ice.

My Daddy's voice sounded so old. "The Sheriff called and said there's been an accident. You need to get dressed."

"What? I don't understand?"

"Your sister had a wreck-thrown from the car. Hurry, Katherine!"

By the time we got to the hospital, Lisa was gone. The doctors said she suffered a rupture to her pulmonary artery. My sister's beautiful heart was torn, ripped beyond repair.

Lisa hit a wet spot in the road and she always drove too fast. The car flipped, and she was thrown into an open field. I entered the emergency room after my parents left. Mary Anne was home with the babies. Lisa and I were alone. I had never seen a dead person, but it was obvious my sister was gone. There wasn't a scratch on her, but she had that pinched look. She was so white, so still. I leaned over and kissed her on the forehead.

"I love you. You weren't supposed to die," I cried.

I couldn't imagine life without my sweet sister. I wondered how such pain was possible. How could anyone feel so much pain and survive it?

"Who will I talk to now?" I cried, tears blurring my vision of her. I stayed with my sister, holding her and crying until the nurse came to tell me that my parents were waiting.

We didn't get back home until eight the next morning. David was waiting for me. I flew into his arms, sobbing deep sobs that came from somewhere inside me. During the next few hours and days that followed, I felt as though I was outside my body, watching myself go through the motions.

At Lisa's wake, I talked to Ray quite a lot. He was the only one I could talk to. My parents were beyond grief; my mother hysterical and Daddy acting like a vacant-eyed robot. I couldn't bring myself to tell them what I was feeling. David tried to comfort me. He kept saying everything was going to be alright, but I knew things would never be alright again. Only Ray seemed to understand. He talked about the night before the accident and how perfect everything had been -- and then everything changed in an instant.

"The very next day, I'm in the emergency room at Lancaster Memorial Hospital looking down at the body of my dead girlfriend."

I winced when Ray said that.

"Sorry, Katie, but it's hard to believe that one minute everything is great, and the next I'm kissing my Lisa on the lips, telling her I will love her forever, and saying goodbye!"

"I understand, Ray."

"I think you do. You know everything that mattered to me, everything that was important to me has ceased to exist," he said with tears streaming down his face.

I didn't say it would get better. I didn't say anything. I simply hugged him and laid my head on his shoulder and wept.

Chapter Ten

OCTOBER 28, 1963

The death of my sister was something I would never get over. The hurt lessened with time and changed into a dull ache instead of a sharp pain. But I would always ache for my sister's company, for our late night conversations. What bothered me most was forgetting the sound of her voice. Everything else I remembered- her face, the laughter, the hugs. It hurt my heart that Quentin and Daniel would never know Lisa.

I tried to keep her alive by reminiscing, but Daddy would tear up and leave the room whenever I mentioned her. His drinking got worse for a while. The boys, thankfully, brought Daddy back to us. It was the boys and David and my friendship with Ray that got me through the worst of it. But I was forever altered. The specter of death was never far from my thoughts.

I stuck pretty close to home after the accident, except for quiet dinners with David. Mary Anne and Terry married in late August. It was a small family gathering, unlike her previous weddings which had been large and circus-like. When school started, I skipped all the things I had previously loved about the fall season-football games, pep rallies and the county fair. I know it must have disappointed David. After all, he was quarterback, and I wasn't at the games to support him. He never complained.

Betsy's upcoming cookout would be the first non-family event I had attended since Lisa's death. I dreaded the whole thing, but David and Betsy insisted that I come. I couldn't disappoint my best friend, plus David had been so patient with me for so long. I knew he was probably tired of the quiet dinners, and a party would be fun, at least for him.

Betsy invited Ray and I insisted that he come with David and me. Ray was completely shattered by the accident. Both Ray's family and mine had tried to help, but nothing seemed to pull him out of his sadness for very long. It was always there, just beneath the surface. In the months and days that followed, Ray told me he lived in a fog. He did what was expected of him, but none of it mattered.

"I can't get excited about college. In fact, I can't imagine going to Vanderbilt or getting a college degree. When it was time to register for the fall semester, I refused to go and told my parents I would go in the spring."

"Ray, you have to get a degree. You can't work for NASA without it," I insisted.

"Katie, nothing matters, not even working for NASA. Babe, when I'm not taking long walks in the woods, I'm at home staring at the walls, thinking of my Lisa. Only you help, Katie. At least with you, I can do what no one else is willing to do -- share memories of Lisa."

I knew our talks helped both of us, but I also knew it was time we both started the healing process. For that reason, I was glad Ray decided to go to the cookout. Like me, it was his first non-family event. On the way to Betsy's, Ray dropped a bombshell.

"Katherine, I got something to tell you and I hope you support me in this."

"What's up Ray?" I asked, fearful of the answer.

"I've joined the Marines; in fact, I've just come from the recruitment office."

"What!" I exclaimed, not believing what I was hearing.

"I leave for Parris Island in two weeks."

"Ray, why in God's name…what in the world possessed you?"

"What's wrong with the Marines?"

"What's wrong with college, with Vanderbilt?" I asked, sick with the knowledge that college was no longer part of the plan.

"I'm not ready for college. I can't concentrate. The Marines will give me something to do until I figure things out. Katie, you know when I signed my name on the dotted line, I felt calm, almost peaceful. I haven't felt that way in a long time."

"Ray, have you lost your mind? What if something happens? God forbid you get wounded."

Ray smiled, shook his head and replied, "We're not at war. I'll probably end up in Germany and play tourist for several years." I started to mention the Cuban Missile Crisis, and what we had gone through the year before, but David interrupted.

"Katie, its Ray's choice and it's done. No point in discussing it."

After that, we drove in silence, but I felt as if I had swallowed another block of ice. It was the way I felt the night Lisa died. That fear and apprehension was present when I said good-bye to Ray two weeks later. Ray's family, my family, and David went to the bus station in Jackson to see Ray off as he left for Parris Island. I hugged him and made him promise to write.

"You better write every day. I mean it, dammit," I insisted.

"Okay," he laughed. "I promise, every day."

In his first letter to me, Ray said that as he took one last look out of the bus window, it was me he saw smiling at him and waving furiously. He told me that he didn't miss Lancaster; that Parris Island was a relief from all the memories. He indicated the only thing he really missed was talking to me every day. He said his letters would be a proper substitute for those talks; that I would still be his sounding board.

We arrived early to help Betsy with last minute preparations. Her back yard was festively decorated in orange and black streamers. White lights strung from various trees and bushes marked the path from the barbecue pit to the playroom, which substituted as a combination dance floor and dining area for the soon-to-be arriving guests.

The party was a huge success. At least sixty people showed up, and David was very attentive. Even Ray seemed to have a good time. David and I slow danced to "I Can't Stop Loving You". As we danced, I pressed closer. I could feel his heart pounding in rhythm with mine. I wanted to crawl inside his skin, become part of him. I couldn't get close enough. A part of me wanted to draw closer than humanly possible. The intensity of my feelings frightened me. I pulled back and realized David was aroused.

Later, after giving Ray a ride home, we drove to a hill overlooking the town and parked the car at its edge. As David turned off the ignition, he pulled me close and kissed me full on the mouth. His intent was unmistakable. For a moment I lingered, then pulled away, again terrified by the intensity of my feelings. I visibly shook. David immediately understood.

"Katie, we've been together long enough and I've been patient. But it hasn't been easy. If we finish what we just started, I can't guarantee it won't go beyond a few kisses."

"I think we better stop," I mumbled in a voice barely audible.

David was silent for a moment then said, "Let's go home, Katie."

We held hands but said little on the way home. When we arrived, David walked me to the door, kissed me softly on the forehead and swiftly left. As I let myself in with a key to the kitchen door and quietly crept through the sleeping house, I thought about what had just happened. Shaken and angry with myself over my cowardice, my mind was a jumble of confused emotions. Each time I began to drift off to sleep, my thoughts awakened me. My mind racing, sleep was all but impossible.

Still groggy from lack of sleep, I called my best friend.

"There must have been a full moon last night because my party sure stirred things up," giggled Betsy.

"How's that?" I yawned.

"Doug danced every dance with me, and you and David were getting pretty hot and heavy. I thought we were going to have to hose y'all down."

"Well, nothing happened, if that's what you're wondering," I said pulling the bed covers up to my chin.

"What a pity."

"I'm not ready, Betsy," I snapped.

"Sorry."

"Forgive me. It's just I'm confused. I want him so much it scares me. I'm afraid I'll be lost if I let go."

"Katherine, that's just crazy."

"I know, but I'm just not ready."

"Then don't do it until you are," advised Betsy.

"That's all well and good, but David's not going to wait forever." Not wanting to discuss it further, I changed the subject.

"Tell me about Doug."

"He asked me to the midnight show."

"That's fantastic. What are you going to wear?" I asked, suddenly awake.

"I don't know, maybe the yellow sundress. What do you think?"

As we continued our conversation, generously peppered with high-pitched giggles, I realized that this was a new experience for my friend. Doug was about to become her first boyfriend. The fact that he was a gentile added another dimension to the situation. Betsy's mother was Jewish, her father Christian. They met during World War II. Her mother was a nurse in a field hospital that her father was transferred to after his leg was injured in the Battle of the Bulge. Shortly after VE Day, they were married, and Chris Graham took his New Jersey bride home to Lancaster to build a house and settle into his family business.

Betsy was an only child and a great deal of attention was lavished on her. She was given piano lessons, dancing lessons, art lessons, riding lessons; the list was endless. Betsy excelled at everything. She had her mother's exotic good looks and her father's keen intelligence. It appeared the world was at her feet, but I knew better. My friend carried the burden of being different in a place that wasn't friendly to those who strayed from the norm.

This otherness was exacerbated by the early lessons of childhood. By the time she was ten, Betsy had seen grisly pictures of Nazi concentration camps that her father's company had taken on their march to Berlin. Her mother had told of relatives, cousins, aunts and great-uncles that died in camps scattered throughout Germany, Austria and Poland. When she was twelve, the nightmares began. They grew in number and intensity as Betsy passed through her teen years. They were always the same: Nazi soldiers dragging her from the comfort and safety of her home into the terror of the streets and certain death.

I was all too familiar with Betsy's damaged psyche. It made me angry at the good people of Lancaster and fearful for my friend.

But now it didn't seem to matter. After the party, Betsy and Doug were inseparable. They went on picnics. They rode horses by the levee and spent their evenings holding hands in the show, going to dances in the Delta, and necking in Doug's car. By their third week together, Doug gave Betsy his L Club ring. I remember when she called me with the news.

"Guess what!"

"I can't, what's up?" I said absentmindedly, concentrating more on painting my toenails than the conversation.

"Doug gave me his ring!"

I put down the polish and exclaimed, "Oh, Betsy, that's great!"

"A year ago, who would have thought, you and David and me and Doug?"

"I'm happy for you. But things aren't so great for me," I said. I knew that I was stealing my friend's thunder, but I needed to talk about David.

"I thought everything was super between you two."

"I'm seriously worried. He isn't calling like he used to. And everything has to be done in groups."

"What do you mean?" asked Betsy.

"We're never alone. Have you noticed, even our dates are a group thing. Either we double with you and Doug or some other couple."

"You need to talk to David. Ask him what's going on."

"I'm afraid. What if he wants to break up?" I asked, almost choking on the words.

"It's better for you to know. You can't go on like this."

"I couldn't stand it if I lost him," I said, my eyes beginning to water.

"You won't," promised Betsy.

NOVEMBER 21, 1963

After Betsy's party, I made an effort to socialize more and do things David wanted to do. Despite the obvious change in him, I didn't confront David. Things didn't get any better. Everything came to a head in November. We were at Angie's, a local eatery specializing in fried shrimp and lemon ice-box pie. Despite the jukebox, a concession to those under eighteen, Angie's was more upscale than the Blue Bird Diner or the local drive-in. The restaurant was populated with round tables covered in satin tablecloths. The walls were painted a light-colored mauve, and small decorative lamps were placed on each table. Oil paintings and watercolors by local artists adorned the center wall of the restaurant, an innovation ahead of its time but very popular. After we were seated, I began talking about the President, something I did a lot of in those days. Little Richard was blaring on the jukebox, and I was shouting to be heard over the music.

"With John Kennedy in the White House, anything's possible," I screamed.

"You idolize him, don't you?"

"Yes, I guess I do," I answered, dipping my shrimp in the remoulade sauce. "He's so handsome. It's nice to have a cute President," I giggled, "not like bald-headed Ike!"

David rolled his eyes.

"But seriously," I continued, "President Kennedy makes me believe everyone can make a difference. You know, change things, real peace and people living together without hating each other."

"Katie, is that realistic?"

"I don't know, it…" I stopped in midsentence. I felt cold; a shudder ran through me.

David looked puzzled and asked, "What's wrong?"

"I feel like someone's walking over my grave." The shudder turned into a visible shake.

David, obviously concerned, asked me again what was wrong.

"I don't know. I have this awful feeling; I can't explain it."
I reached for a glass of water and the shaking began to subside.
"I'm being dramatic. Let's talk about something else."

"We need to talk about us."

"Okay," I said, anxiously dreading the outcome.

David took my hands in his and said, "Katie, you aren't there
for me. I know the last six months have been hard, but I need
you."

"I'm sorry, David."

Looking squarely into my eyes, David continued. "And it's
not just that. You blow hot and cold, and it's driving me crazy.
You're a tease and I can't handle it."

"David, I'm not. Not really. It's just that I get scared," I
explained.

"Well, you better deal with it, because I can't take it much
longer." David's voice had a definite edge to it.

"Please, David, try to understand." My face now registered
the fear I was feeling.

"I do," David responded. "But you've got to understand that
things have to change."

"They will, I promise."

The next day all hell broke loose. It was the class period
after lunch and Principal Nevin's voice came over the ancient
loud speaker. All I heard was President, motorcade, and Dallas.
In less than an hour, President Kennedy was dead and nobody
knew who did it. We heard that the Governor of Texas and the
Vice-President were dead too. We heard it was the Russians.
Everyone was scared, even our teachers.

After school, I went straight home and turned on the TV.
My parents joined me. It wasn't until the six o'clock news that
we knew it was a lone gunman, or so we thought. As Jackie left
Air Force One with Bobby, Mama said, "She's in shock."

"How do you know?" I asked, wanting to cry but refusing to
in front of Mama.

"Her eyes are unfocused. She looks like she's in a trance,"
said Mama.

As Daddy turned up the volume, he expressed sorrow for Caroline and John John. "They're too young to lose their Daddy. It's a crying shame."

David called in the middle of Walter Cronkite, wanting to go to the Friday night basketball game. I told him to go with his friends, and I spent the weekend in front of the TV. The death of the President rattled me. As long as John Kennedy was in the White House I felt safe. I no longer felt that way. I couldn't imagine the world continuing to orbit on its axis. Why didn't everything come to a screeching halt? My President was dead and so was my sister. How could life go on as though nothing had happened? After that I concentrated on collecting Special Edition magazines memorializing the President and starting a scrapbook about JFK. I pretty much ignored David. It was a month before I agreed to go to another basketball game. Afterwards we went to Angie's for a late snack. I could tell David was upset. As we got out of the car, David slammed the door and walked ahead of me into the restaurant. As I ran to catch up with him, I called out, "What's wrong?"

"We'll talk about it inside."

We sat at a table near the window. I noticed the traffic was thinning out and the windows were beginning to steam from the winter cold. As we looked at the menu, David let me know what was up. "Katherine, I think we need to spend some time apart. Maybe see other people."

I felt as though someone had kicked me in the stomach.

"David, please…"

"I'm serious. I think it's for the best, until you get over your obsession with all things dead."

"I'm really sorry…"

David interrupted again in an attempt to drive his point home. "It's not forever. I just need a break and you need to work things out."

"I'll try, things will get better," I said, my voice breaking. David's face turned red and he yelled at me, "No, Katie, we need a break!"

I excused myself from the table and practically ran to the bathroom. When I returned, my dinner had arrived. I took two bites and asked David to take me home. The ride was swift and silent. David didn't get out of the car. As I opened the kitchen door, I could hear him screeching off, probably leaving tire marks halfway down the street. I was numb and strangely detached from my surroundings. I felt something wet on my cheeks and realized it was tears.

Chapter Eleven
DECEMBER 1, 1963

Christmas was upon us, but I wasn't in the mood for anything other than tears, accusations, and suspicions. Things had been going so well since the birth of the twins. My daughters were thrilled with their little brothers. It was an idyllic time. Mary Anne was in love again, and everything seemed to be going well with David and Katherine, despite my apprehensions. Even Tom and I were getting along better. The days before the birth of my twins, Tom and I began to connect. We talked in ways we never had before. We talked about the pain he caused me. The affair, the drinking, the unexplained disappearances were bad, but none of it hurt as much as the verbal abuse. From the start of our marriage, my husband harped on my lack of taste and breeding, my ignorance, and my lack of education. I remember one conversation in particular that took place after attending a dinner party at Tom's parents' house. As we drove the two miles from their place to our starter home, Tom accused me of being completely devoid of proper skills.

"Pat, your persona is wooden and unresponsive. Whenever we go out in public, you clam up."

His critique reminded me of a film director dressing down an actor for not properly playing her part. As we turned into our driveway, Tom continued, "You know your inadequacies are affecting my business opportunities. How can you expect me to entertain clients when you don't have the slightest idea how to be a proper wife, much less a proper hostess? I realize your background didn't prepare you for much, but you should try for both our sakes!"

I later told my husband that I understood his tirades were fueled by alcohol, but they still hurt. In one of those late-night talks when everyone else was asleep, I told Tom just how much his remarks hurt me.

"Your barrage of insults made me feel inadequate as a wife, a homemaker, even as a woman. After that, I tried to become someone you would be proud of."

"Really? I didn't realize …"

"I bought fashion magazines and studied them like schoolbooks to learn how to dress properly. I went to the local library and checked out books on interior design. Tom, I devoured all I could find on etiquette, especially Emily Post. I did everything possible to become a lady of class and taste, but nothing pleased you. I guess I will always be inferior to you."

"Pat, I'm truly sorry. I've been a pompous ass. I had no idea. And no, you're not the inferior one. You're not the alcoholic who was a major disappointment to your parents."

"Tom, why did you drink and gamble? When did it start? Do you realize we've been married more years than I can count and there's still a lot I don't know about you?"

Tom leaned over, took my hand in his, and told me his story.

"I've always lived in the shadow of my brother, Jack. As you know, I'm the third of four boys. Robbie and Garrett left while I was still in grammar school and settled in St. Louis. They hardly ever returned to Lancaster after that."

"Well, naturally," I said. "They have families of their own. Robbie's what – ten years older?"

"Yes, and Garrett's eight years older than me, so I was closer to Jack, but that didn't stop me from being jealous."

"Why were you jealous?" I asked, even though I knew the answer.

"My parents doted on Jack. He could do no wrong. My brother was a natural athlete – the star punter on the football team, the starting pitcher on the baseball team and, of course, the best player on Lancaster's tennis team. I was okay at sports, but nothing like Jack."

"Tom, you're smart and successful. Why do you feel inferior to Jack?" I asked.

"Yes, I'm smart," he answered. "But not as smart as Jack. He maintained a straight-A average through high school, as well as the University of Tennessee.

I, on the other hand, never earned anything above a C at Ole Miss."

"I'm sorry, Tom," I said, squeezing his hand.

"I could never live up to my parent's expectations. I would never be as good as Jack in their eyes."

"When did the drinking start?" I asked.

"The drinking and gambling started not long after my sixteenth birthday. The gambling gave me a thrill; I had beginner's luck. Finally, there was something I could do better than Jack. Plus, the drinking washed away the sense of inferiority. Both vices got out of hand quickly. I almost ran Dad's car into a tree. My allowance didn't begin to cover the gambling debts I was accumulating."

"Vincent said everything changed when Chrissie came into your life."

"Yes, that's right. She transferred from St. Michael's to Lancaster High the beginning of our sophomore year. Since she was a tall, striking blond, I noticed her immediately, but it took a year to get her to go out with me. Do you really want to know about this?"

"Yes," I answered. I knew it would be painful to hear, but I still wanted to know.

"She refused to take me seriously until I quit what she called my 'carousing'. I fell hard and tried to be everything she wanted me to be. Not only did I straighten up my act, I hit the books as well. I went from middle C's to an A in everything except physics." He laughed and said, "I earned a B+ in that course."

"I guess your parents were relieved," I interjected.

"Yes, at first my family was happy, but that happiness became alarm near the end of my senior year in high school."

"Why alarm?"

"We wanted to get married and we didn't want to wait four years. I knew my parents and hers, too, would never give us permission so we planned to elope the night of our senior prom. It was a midnight till dawn dance. No one would suspect anything until well after sun-up. By then it would be too late for Mom and Dad to intervene."

"So what happened?"

"I picked Chrissie up around ten o'clock that night and instead of heading for the dance, we drove toward Alabama."

"How far did you get?"

"As we crossed the state line, I saw the blue lights. We got a police escort back to Lancaster."

"Did you see her after that? I mean that summer?"

"No, not for a long, long time. Our parents kept us separated the entire summer. I went to Ole Miss in the fall and proceeded to drink my way through college until I joined the service not long before the Japs bombed Pearl Harbor."

"I remember you telling me you were in the Navy."

"Yes, on an aircraft carrier in the Pacific and I loved it. But my service in the Navy was cut short due to my eardrum injury."

"Tom, you remember when you told me your affair with Chrissie started early in our marriage? Is that true?"

"Yes, it started not long after you and I were married. Chrissie hooked up with some Catholic boy from Vicksburg, hand-picked by her parents and well on his way to becoming a doctor. You know, my parents never wrote me about Chrissie's wedding. Fred broke the news in one of his letters to me."

"And you never forgave them," I added.

"I guess you're right. Anyway, about two months after we married, I ran into Chrissie at the local cleaners. The affair started then and it didn't end until the day of Lee's birthday party. So now you know everything."

"Almost," I said. "I just have one more question. Is Chrissie the reason you went on that ten-day drunk in Birmingham?"

"Yes. I ran into Chrissie's husband. Martin had his suspicions about me and his wife. We exchanged words and, when Chrissie found out, she broke it off. The break-up lasted about three months, long enough to send me into a bout of drinking and the road trip to Birmingham."

Our talks about Tom's past lead to many more late night talks. As a result, Tom began to change, and so did I.

My husband was ecstatic over the birth of his sons. He took an active role in their care, even changing dirty diapers. He went out of his way to please me. Tom insisted on a night out once a week, just for the two of us. He would take me to dinner and a show. Sometimes we would go dancing at the King Edward Hotel in Jackson. He was actually courting me again, just like he did prior to our marriage.

I remember one night in June, when we were dancing under the stars on top of the King Edward, Tom pulled me close and asked, "Are you happy, Pat?"

"Do you mean in general or at this particular moment?"

"Just answer the question," said Tom, somewhat impatiently.

"Yes, Tom," I answered. "I'm happier than I've been in a long time."

"I hope I'm somewhat responsible for that."

"Yes, you are. You've really been trying since the twins were born and it hasn't gone unnoticed. I appreciate you being there for them and me and …"

"And what?" he asked.

"The non-drinking and, of course, the other …"

"You mean Chrissie?"

"Yes, that," I responded.

"I meant what I said, Pat. No more Chrissie," Tom assured me.

"Let's change the subject to something more pleasant," I said, not feeling entirely comfortable with the subject matter.

As Tom twirled me around the dance floor, I told him what else made me happy.

"Our girls seem to be in a good place, even Katherine."

My husband gently admonished me and asked, "Maybe, then, you'll give her a break?"

"Okay, okay. I'll try. It's just I can't agree with everything you and Katherine believe in, and the way she talks scares me,

Tom!"

"It's her life," he argued. "She's almost grown, Pat. You're going to have to start letting her live it!"

"I know, but she's not grown yet, and if I don't rein her in …"

"Pat, give her some room, just a little, okay?"

I smiled at my husband and said, "Okay."

As the music stopped, Tom leaned over and kissed me softly on the lips. I relaxed and began to believe that everything was going to be alright. God wasn't going to punish me for what happened with Fred.

It all came crashing down with the death of Lisa. The very fabric of my family was ripped apart. The grief we all felt was almost palpable. You could feel it in the air. It hung there like a dark cloud that wouldn't go away. It wasn't long before I began to smell liquor on Tom's breath. He said the mere mention of Lisa's name caused the grief to close in on him and almost destroy his sanity. "What about my sanity," I asked him in one of the many escalating fights between us.

Tom said there was no reasoning with me, and he was right. I became overly protective of Katherine, terrified that something would happen to her. If she was five minutes late coming home from school, I would go crazy. The more Tom tried to calm me down, the angrier and more vicious I would become. There was a rage in me, an anger and bitterness that colored everything I did.

The anger seemed to grow each day. I was angry at Tom, at life, and most of all, God. Since my Lisa's death, my rage threatened to overwhelm me and my entire family

The Christmas of 1963 for my family was like the gathering of the walking wounded. We were poster children for the dysfunctional family before the term became popular. Mama and Daddy hardly ever talked. When they did, it ended in a fight. I marveled at the fact that they had gotten married in the first place. Their backgrounds and personalities were so different. Daddy was from a prominent Southern family whose lineage dated back to Bonnie Prince Charlie. Mama's parents were dirt poor farmers from West Virginia. During the Depression, they barely carved out an existence.

Mama was always afraid, even more since Lisa died. Whenever I left the house, I had to check with Mama. If I was ten minutes late coming home, Mama went berserk. She cried, screamed, and threatened. If Daddy tried to calm her down, Mama would turn on him. Sometimes those fights got really nasty and, more often than not, I was privy to them. Many of these fights were about me, but not always. Two weeks before Christmas, they got into it over the twins. Mama and I were in the den decorating the Christmas tree when Daddy stormed in.

Red-faced, his blue eyes darkened with rage, he screamed at Mama, "Pat, have you lost your damned mind?"

"Good afternoon to you too," responded Mama, not looking up as she placed an ornament on the tree.

"Why, why did you do it? What possessed you to fire the twins' nurse?" asked Daddy, obviously beside himself with anger and frustration.

"She wasn't watching them close enough. What if something happened, Tom…?"

"This is the fourth nurse you've fired in two months," interrupted Daddy.

"How many nurses are you planning on going through? Do you believe there's an unlimited supply of them?"

"I'm just trying to protect my babies from harm."

"No, Pat, you've lost it," screamed Daddy. "You've gone off the deep end!"

"It's really amusing how you've suddenly become the doting father since I've given you sons. You couldn't give a damn about the girls. You were never around when they were babies; too busy drinking. Poor Lisa is lying in her grave and you've already forgotten her. All you can think about is a nurse for your boys!" said Mama, snarling and spewing out her venom.

Daddy blanched and screamed back, "You damned bitch. I love my girls and you're not the only one grieving over Lisa's death. I'm gonna hire the next nurse, and if you fire her, you can just do without help. Do you understand?" he screamed.

"Yes, Sir," Mama screamed back sarcastically.

With that, Daddy left the house, slamming the door behind him. He didn't come back until long after midnight. Mama didn't seem to notice.

I felt guilty, somehow responsible for their fights. I tried hard to do everything right, but it was never enough for Mama. At seventeen, I thought Mama was the enemy. It wasn't until much later that I discovered that Daddy played on Mama's insecurities and made her feel inferior. Daddy sincerely believed anyone who was directly related to him had superior genes. It wasn't that he was an ordinary bigot. He didn't feel that whites were better than Negroes. He felt that everyone, whatever their color, was less than the Boyd family and their predecessors. He would joke about it, but I knew deep down he really meant it. And, of course, Mama wasn't a Boyd, not really.

She came to Mississippi in the 1940's. She followed her fiancé to Camp Shelby during World War II. He was killed after being shipped to the Pacific. After his death, Mama moved to the central part of the state to find work. She ended up as a teller in Daddy's bank. Daddy was immediately taken by Mama's exotic good looks. People often said she looked like Snow White, with the dark hair and pale skin. Mama had a quiet dignity that surfaced when she was out in public. I later realized it was a cover up for the painful shyness she suffered from all her life. For all of Mama's shyness, Daddy was very outgoing. In fact, it was said he never met a stranger. Within a month of meeting, they were serious about each other. Daddy's parents didn't really approve, at least not at first. Mama later said that's probably why he married her -- sheer rebellion on his part.

It wasn't too long after my parents married that they both realized how little they had in common. It was then that Daddy's drinking got worse. He had been a heavy drinker in college, but had tapered off once he started working at the bank. But after he married, Daddy's drinking didn't lessen until my sisters were born. One thing that didn't seem to change was the way Daddy needled Mama and her angry reaction to his sarcasm.

And then there was my sister, Mary Anne, who came home for Christmas with her new husband in tow. Her appearance was shocking. Mary Anne's lovely figure had lost its roundness; her skin took on a sickly pall. My sister's raven hair was brittle and lifeless. This was unusual because my sister was fastidious about her appearance, especially her hair. She brushed it 100 times a day and used special hair products that were ordered from New York. It was not like my sister to let herself go. The most frightening thing about her appearance was the vacant, glazed over look in her eyes. My sister's behavior was as shocking as her looks. She said very little and, when she did speak, it was in incomplete sentences. She tended to slur her words. When my parents asked what was wrong with her, my sister explained that her doctor had temporarily prescribed Valium for her nerves, due to Lisa's death.

At night after everyone had gone to bed, I heard Mary Anne quietly sobbing in her room. After several nights of this, I knocked on her bedroom door. When no one answered, I opened the door. I saw Terry leaning over the bed urging my sister to take another Valium.

I, like the others, was into my own pain. None of us talked

about Lisa. It was a subject we never broached, an unspoken taboo. I was grieving over the loss of David as well. The one person I could always talk to about anything, who always made things better, was Lisa. Many times during that Christmas holiday, I went to her room for one of our heart to hearts only to realize over and over again that Lisa was gone. Each time, it felt like someone had knocked the breath out of me.

After Christmas came New Year's. Betsy and Doug insisted that I go to a neighbor's New Year's party with them. After we left the party, we stopped by the Blue Bird Diner for a late snack. We hadn't been there ten minutes when David walked in, hand in hand with Patrice Drew. The girl that gazed lovingly into David' eyes was a sophomore beauty and a member of the homecoming court that year. My heart sank as David guided Patrice in the direction of our booth. As they came closer, I could see David's L Club ring dangling from a gold chain around Patrice's flawless neck.

"Hi, everybody, I guess y'all know Patrice."

As David spoke, he watched me intently. It was obvious that he wanted to see my reaction.

"Yes," I said. "How are you Patrice?"

Patrice leaned over and whispered, "Katherine, I'm glad you and David are such good friends. I know that must have meant a lot after Lisa's death. And I want you to know, I want y'all to continue to be good friends."

"Really," I said, as the anger in me began to rise.

"Yes, as a matter of fact, I told him so." Patrice's smugness was evident in every word she spoke.

I wanted to throttle David for what he was doing. I wondered why he was so insensitive. Didn't he realize what he was doing to me? With as much dignity as I could muster, I gave some excuse for leaving. My last words before I practically broke into a run while leaving the diner were, "Great to see you both, and oh, by the way, Happy New Year."

That night I sobbed myself into a fitful sleep. The next morning, as I stumbled toward the hall bathroom, I noticed something lying in the center of the hallway. It was my sister.

A pool of blood encased her raven hair. I then saw blood on a small table in the hall; it was obvious she had hit her head as she fell. I screamed for help and tried to wake her, but I couldn't. I heard the sirens coming closer and I wondered if I would lose Mary Anne as well.

My sister survived, but just barely. She had swallowed six Valium and had her stomach pumped, among other things. Her near-death united my parents. Daddy supported Mama throughout the terrible ordeal. Their previous disagreements gave way to fear for Mary Anne and to a resolve to help her. They insisted upon treatment for Mary Anne, despite Terry's resistance. He said his wife was his responsibility and my parents needed to butt out. This led to a screaming match between Mama and Terry. Daddy literally had to get between them. It was obvious to everyone that Terry was part of the problem. My parents realized Terry had a fondness for pills, especially Dexedrine and Valium. Mama's insistence and not too subtle threats wore Terry down. My sister went into treatment far from home. Terry denied that anything was really wrong with his wife or himself. Just an accident, he said. Mary Anne had simply miscounted, forgotten how many pills she had taken.

In the winter of 1964, there was plenty of denial to go around. No one talked about daddy's drinking, which he had kept in check while the twins were little. Mama refused to deal with the effects of Lisa's death. After Mary Anne's overdose, she got more protective and more possessive. The twins were never out of her sight, and she watched me like a hawk. My only relief came from Betsy and the letters I received from Ray. I remember how happy I was to receive Ray's letter and learn he had made several friends. For the first time in a long time, he seemed happy. I read and re-read his letter until I practically had it memorized.

Dear Katie:

Basic training wasn't as bad as I thought it would be. I made friends with two guys from Kentucky. One is a twenty-year-old coal miner from Morganfield. His name is Luther, but we call him Luke. He's always smiling – a practical joker whose sense of fun is infectious. Luke has worked in the mines since graduating from high school. He told me he didn't want to die with coal dust in his lungs so he joined the Marines. Uncle Sam will pay for college, something Luke can't afford on his own. He wants to be an architect, just like Frank Lloyd Wright. He has a girl, his high school sweetheart. They want to get married and start a family but, of course, all that takes money, financial security. Luke figures a few years in the Marines will give him the security he needs for the future.

My other friend is an amateur boxer from Madisonville. Bobby is quieter, more introspective than Luke. He's been on his own since seventeen. Boxing paid the bills. Like Luke, Bobby wants to go to college and then to law school.

Katie, I know this sounds crazy, but Parris Island was a relief. While others complained about the heat, the drill sergeant screaming in our ears, and being homesick -- I didn't. I loved boot camp. I concentrated on the drills and learned to handle a gun. I've been so busy, I didn't have time to think – so tired at the end of the day, there were no dreams or nightmares about Lisa.

We've just gotten our orders. All three of us are being shipped out to Okinawa, Japan.

Got to go -- will write soon.

Love, Ray

What Ray's letter didn't say was Japan was the stopping off spot for their destination, Vietnam. My next letter from Ray described the country that none of us knew much about, but its name and the horror of it would soon be permanently embedded in America's collective memory, thanks to the nightly news. I had begun to hear things about Vietnam that contradicted what was being reported by politicians in Washington. I told Ray what I heard and asked him about it. He, too, had heard things from fellow soldiers whose relatives back home began to enlighten their brothers, sons and sweethearts. Ray's letter not only described the history of Vietnam but a lot more.

Dear Katie:

> *By the time I enlisted, I, like most Americans, knew little about Vietnam. As I entered the military transport headed for Japan, I knew nothing about the Vietnamese fight for independence and freedom from the shackles of French Colonial rule, a fight that started as early as the 1900's and ended with the ouster of the French in 1954. I simply thought it was a civil war between communist north and the democratic south. I had been told that South Vietnam had been wrongly invaded by the north and that we were trying to help the south fight off the advances of the Communists and prevent the entire area from falling under Communist rule, orchestrated by Moscow and Peking. I listened to the nightly news and read articles in various magazines and newspapers that claimed the domino theory applied to Vietnam. Look what happened to Eastern Europe at the end of World War II, they reasoned. All those magazines and newspapers said if we didn't take a stand and give aid and assistance to the South, then all of Asia, and God knows what else, would fall to Communist rule.*
>
> *What I didn't know was when the French were ousted from Vietnam, a cease-fire between the two*

nations temporarily divided Vietnam between the North and South until a nation-wide election could be held and the people of Vietnam could decide what kind of government they wanted. The United States, afraid that the South would go the way of the North, urged the South to establish an independent government. We would support the South with aid and military advisers. Unfortunately, the new South Vietnam was governed by Ngo Dinh Diem. His rule had nothing to do with democracy and everything to do with military dictatorship and nepotism. He and his brother have since been assassinated, and now another dictator is ruling the South. It's a shame since it's such a beautiful country. You ought to see the beaches. I'm used to swimming in the muddy-looking liquid of the Mississippi River. The blue-green water of the Pacific Ocean is a marvel to me. It reminds me of the west Florida vacations my family used to take every summer. I couldn't wait to unpack and stake out my room in our rented condo and race to the nearest beach. The white sands and blue waters of Destin, along with a dinner of soft-shell crabs, was always the highlight of our annual trip.

The one thing I don't like is the stifling heat. Naturally, growing up in Mississippi, I'm used to the heat and humidity. But this is different. The minute I stepped off a C-141 cargo jet, the heat hit me hard. It's like being in a sauna – a wet, hot heat that makes it hard to breathe. I don't think I will ever get used to it.

Got to go – more training to do.

Love, Ray

Besides Ray's letters, Betsy tried to keep my mind off David. She insisted that I come to her house to watch the Beatles on Ed Sullivan. Doug was there, and Betsy's mother provided the comic relief. She sang along with the TV "I Want to Hold Your Hand" and told us why she liked the Beatles more than Elvis.

"They're just adorable, such nice young men-not like that vulgar Elvis who shakes his hips at you."

I laughed so hard I cried. After that Betsy insisted I go to the movies with her and Doug. I felt like a third wheel, but Doug also insisted. I even went to basketball games with them. It was at one of the home games that I saw David enter the gym with Patrice. When he put his arm around her waist, I ran to the bathroom. Waves of nausea hit me. As my body shook with uncontrolled spasms, my friend entered the bathroom. After I finished throwing up, Betsy handed me a wet towel. I raised my head from the toilet and asked, "What am I going to do? I can't stand to see him with her. I feel like I've been kicked in the stomach."

My friend tried to comfort me with a lie. "Katherine, it will get better with time, I promise."

"No, it won't. I'll never stop loving him. Not ever."

"You need to start dating. Get back in the game," suggested Betsy.

With tears streaming down my face, I said, "You don't understand do you? No one does. There isn't anyone I want to date."

"Katherine, please," pleaded Betsy, "You've got to pull out of this. Please try!"

"Okay, okay, I'll try," I lied.

After that, I quit going out altogether. I missed the best part of my senior year, the dances, swimming parties, and barbecues. I even missed our graduation dance. Anything was better than seeing David with Patrice. I spent the summer before college babysitting the twins and watching soaps. Like the summer of 1963, my world was forever altered by events I couldn't control or even predict.

JUNE 26, 1964

After treatment, my sister came home for a month, but ended up staying the entire summer. Mary Anne's appearance had improved dramatically. Her hair had its old luster, and she had gained back most of the weight she had lost. But her looks were deceiving. Mary Anne was not herself. She took little interest in anything and said even less. Mama, who had been toying with the idea of redoing parts of the house, especially after the twins were born, decided it was time to remodel. She enlisted Mary Anne's help. It turned out to be one of Mama's better ideas. If there was one thing Mary Anne enjoyed more than shopping for clothes, it was redecorating. Slowly, my sister's confident and very opinionated self began to emerge. I was now grateful for the little things about Mary Anne that had previously aggravated me. It appeared my sister was finally on the road to recovery, or at least that's the way it appeared in the summer of 1964.

The twins kept me busy that summer. The two were at that toddler stage and into everything that wasn't nailed down. Daniel was particularly fascinated with loud sounds and crashing objects. He became quite adept at throwing breakable objects. Even his dinner plate and bottle were not spared this exercise in infant hijinks. While surveying the ungodly mess from the vantage point of his high chair, he would gleefully screech, "Did ya' broke it?"

Quentin adopted a less physical method of expressing himself. The tongue was and would always be his most reliable tool and most effective weapon. When he was only four, he stubbornly resisted the commands of his swimming instructor, by declaring he most certainly did not have to breathe under water. "All I have to do is die and pay taxes." When he wasn't shocking adults with his vocabulary and pint-sized philosophy, he would cling to the hem of my skirt with two fingers, well hidden from prying eyes by the protective and solid presence of his older sister. The twins made that difficult summer before college bearable.

What was less comforting was the tone of Ray's letters. They were no longer full of news about his friends from Kentucky or the beauty of the country he now inhabited.

Dear Katie:

> *As you know, I received a lot of training at Parris Island and then in Japan, more training, but no amount of training could prepare me for the heat, the rain, the mud, or the Vietcong or their use of primitive but effective weapons and, of course, the constant fear – not for myself, but for my friends – all those fresh-faced kids who, like myself, grew up on <u>Father Knows Best</u> and Mickey Mouse…*

Ray's next letter was even more alarming.

> *I've been deployed to DANang in the Mekong Delta. After the Gulf of Tonkin Resolution – you know it was in the news – it was Johnson's excuse for escalating the war. Well, anyway, since then a lot more Marines have arrived. There's a lot less advising and more combat. We're no longer military advisers to the South Vietnamese but are fully engaged in the fighting. No more pretense.*
>
> *Not long after I arrived here, we set up base, which is a series of tents on a muddy terrain. Luke and I pulled guard duty. I covered the center and Luke was assigned to the far left side of the base. I pulled duty from twelve midnight until six o'clock the next morning. Except for occasional communications between those of us guarding the perimeters, things were pretty quiet. Too quiet, in fact. I had time to think about the past -- to remember. We were told to watch for anyone crawling or walking and to look in the trees to see if we were being watched. Sometimes I could feel them out there watching and waiting. I*

heard sounds of movement beyond the trees, out there beyond the bushes, just waiting to strike, to do damage and then run …

The letters continued to come over the next couple of years, and each letter was darker than the previous letter I had received from him.

Dear Katie:

More fire-fights. I'll never forget the first one. About twenty of us were doing recon; our Point, Rodger O'Malley from Wisconsin, took a direct hit. His left leg was blown clean off. All a sudden the sky lit up like the Fourth of July, and it was coming from everywhere – the trees, the left and the right. It seemed as if we were surrounded. We returned fire for about twenty minutes, and I thought all of us would meet our maker that day. Miraculously, fifteen of our platoon survived.

After that, I saw a lot worse than Rodger losing his leg. You stop making friends with new arrivals because you don't know who might end up being a mass of blood and pulp the next week or even the next day. I saw a man hanging upside down in a booby-trapped tree impaled on a sharpened stake attached to the tree. Then there are the pitfalls, woven mats covering a hole in the ground disguising the stakes underneath. You have to be on the alert constantly, looking up in the sky to see an enemy who might be in a tree staring down at you.

Always watching your step because you never know what's in front of you, a booby-trap or maybe a land mine…

One letter in particular made me cry. It's the one in which he described the death of his friends.

Katie,

> *Luke stepped on a landmine and there weren't enough
> pieces of him to send home in a body bag. My friend
> who wanted to be an architect was literally blown to
> bits. The night before he died, Luke talked about his
> girl back in Morganfield. He had just received a letter
> from her, and they were both counting the days until
> he could get some R & R in Hawaii. Teresa would
> be there waiting for him. I miss my friend and our
> late night conversations. Things don't seem so desperate
> when you have a friend to share your thoughts with…*

And then came the news of Bobby's death. Ray described a
conversation with Bobby shortly before he died.

> *Lately, my thoughts are full of Lisa. I have visions
> of her; my dreams are packed full of our many talks.
> Somehow, my sweet girl seems to be communicating
> with me. I feel her presence even in my waking hours.
> Bobby noticed the effect all this had on me and he
> mentioned it one night after we both came off guard
> duty. He asked why I was so distracted and warned
> that it wasn't good to be that way out here in the
> boonies. I told him I was thinking about Lisa. It was
> then that Bobby said he would never have a girlfriend;
> not like me and Luke. I laughed it off and reassured
> him that once he got back to the States, he would meet
> someone, probably at school. I told him I wanted to
> be best man at his wedding. The next day, my friend
> died from a single bullet through the heart. Bobby
> was killed securing a piece of land that had been taken
> three weeks before. The irony of it wasn't lost on those
> of us left in my unit…*

That letter filled me with terror for Ray and deep sadness for
his lost friends. More than Ray's physical safety, I feared for his

sanity, his very soul. What would be left of the friend I once knew after he served his tour of duty and came home?

Despite my concern over Ray and my anguish over David, life seemed to be uneventful that summer. The lazy quiet days of summer descended, broken only by the sporadic and frenzied activity of Mama, Mary Anne, and a group of exhausted decorators. The quiet was shattered on Father's Day. After a meal of Daddy's favorite foods and the ritual of opening presents consisting of ties, a robe, and numerous dress shirts, Daddy settled into his favorite chair for an hour of "Bonanza." While Daddy watched the antics of Hoss and Little Joe, three young men were being taken to a place where their young lives would end. The place was called Rock Cut Road, and their names were James, Michael and Andrew.

The lush landscape and the soft sultry Mississippi nights inspired the imaginations of many, and I could be counted among them. I sometimes imagined the dead freely mingling with the exotic animal life that populated the Mississippi swamps. I envisioned the numerous rivers and lakes that crisscrossed one another and decorated Mississippi maps with their blue veins turning scarlet with the blood of so many victims whose deaths were never declared, whose funerals were never held and whose final resting places were muddy rivers, named by the long ago Indians that once inhabited Mississippi territory. James, Michael and Andrew joined these nameless victims in their undisclosed graves, and their story appeared on the noonday news that following Monday.

It was announced that three civil rights workers were missing from their COFO (Council of Federated Organizations) headquarters in Meridian. They had not been seen since they left the area the previous morning to investigate a church burning in Neshoba County. Their names were James Chaney, Michael Schewerner and Andrew Goodman. None were over the age of twenty-five. All were involved in voter registration, and Andrew was part of a student-filled migration to Mississippi, better known as "Freedom Summer." The newscaster said they were only missing, but I knew they were dead. Everyone did, despite public statements to the contrary. A massive manhunt began once their burned out station wagon was discovered in a swamp thirteen miles northeast of Philadelphia.

The news bulletin left me sick with dread. I picked at my food and thought of those three young men. Their youth unnerved me. I remembered when I first heard about "Freedom Summer" earlier that spring. I had wondered about those young college students who were coming south to help with voter registration. I wished I could talk with them and really get to know them. But an entire society built on a culture I no longer understood, not to mention the watchful eyes of my parents, separated me from these young activists. My identification with the three missing men left me weak with sadness and shame. My shame increased as the days flowed into weeks and local politicians treated the disappearance in a cavalier fashion, making jokes about it, the Governor in particular.

Forty-four days later, their bodies were discovered buried in an earthen dam southwest of Philadelphia known as the Old Jolly Farm. At 7:45 p.m. Lancaster time, regular programming at the local television station was interrupted with the news of the discovery of the bodies.

Local officials participated in the recovery of the bodies and transportation of the three to the University Medical Center in Jackson for an official autopsy. As the camera zeroed in on the face of the local deputy sheriff, Daddy astounded us by announcing, "That son of a bitch did it!"

"What are you talking about?" asked Mama.

"The Deputy Sheriff. He's guilty; he was involved in their murders. I'm sure of that."

"Daddy, how could you know that?" I asked.

"He's got a sick nervous look - a guilty look written all over his red neck face," Daddy responded.

"Well, they had no business being down here," said Mama. "I feel for their families, but they had no business being down here where they didn't belong."

I was too sad to get angry with Mama's remarks. I realized many of our neighbors felt just like Mama.

But the irony didn't stop there. Rita Schewerner, the wife of Michael, said the press, the nation, wouldn't have cared if two of the victims hadn't been white. It was then that I realized that Mississippi didn't have a monopoly on prejudice.

When I look back on the summer of 1964, it's not the twins that I think of or even Mary Anne's visit, but the death of three young men, so close to my own age.

Chapter Fourteen
AUGUST 20, 1964

The near death of my second daughter made me realize I still had a lot to lose. Tom and I put up a united front in our effort to save Mary Anne from her drug-induced hell. It's ironic how Lisa's death caused a riff in our fragile relationship. Mary Anne's addiction and near death had the opposite effect; it brought us closer together.

After his initial shock, Tom became someone I could turn to, to lean on when it all got too much to handle. He was my rock, my support system. From the moment Katherine found Mary Anne unconscious and bleeding profusely, Tom took over. His quick thinking probably saved my daughter's life. He got her medical help and under the care of a physician in record time. While we were waiting for Dr. Pierce to tell us if Mary Anne would survive or not, Tom put his arms around me and reassured me that our daughter would be okay.

"Honey, she's going to make it. I just know it."

"How could you know that, Tom," I cried. "I don't think I can stand it if she dies." I put my head in my hands and began to sob.

Tom pulled me close and said, "Pat, Mary Anne is different from Lisa. She was alive when Katie found her. She's young and she's got a strong heart. She's going to make it," he repeated, "and we're going to get her the help she needs."

Suddenly, Dr. Pierce was in the waiting room telling us Mary Anne would pull through. After our initial relief, he brought us back to reality.

"Your daughter needs help. She's seriously addicted and you need to get her treatment as quickly as possible."

Tom got right on it, checking facilities all over the country, and found one in Nebraska that fit Mary Anne's needs. But that didn't solve the problem of Terry. A user himself, he tried to obstruct our attempts to save our daughter. When we tried to convince Mary Anne she needed help, her husband intervened and tried to convince her otherwise. Terry and I almost came to blows. It was Tom that diffused the situation. It all came to a head the weekend after Mary Anne was released from the hospital. Tom was cooking steaks on the grill. I was making the salad and Katherine was setting the table. As I sliced the cucumbers and tomatoes for the salad, Terry walked into the kitchen and announced he and Mary Anne were leaving for New Orleans the next day.

"Are you crazy?" I screamed, "or is it you just don't give a damn about Mary Anne?"

"I don't know what all the fuss is about. Mary Anne just lost count. It wasn't deliberate."

"Yes, she just lost count," I shot back, "and it almost cost my daughter her life. You don't seriously think Mary Anne's okay, do you?"

"Yes, Pat, that's just what I think, and I also think it's none of your business."

With that, I lunged toward Terry. Tom, quick as a flash, stepped in between us and prevented me from striking my son-in-law. If he hadn't entered the kitchen when he did, I probably would have hit Terry. Tom's actions may have prevented me from slapping Terry, but it didn't prevent my verbal assault on my daughter's husband.

"You worthless piece of garbage," I screamed. "You don't want my daughter to get help because you want someone to party with while you abuse drugs. You don't care about anything but the high you get from your pills."

"Tom, you better get your wife under control," yelled Terry.

With that, Tom laughed and said, "No one controls my wife."

Without missing a beat, I continued my tirade. "If you attempt to take my daughter out of this house or prevent her from getting the help she needs, I will have you put under the jail, not in it! Do I make myself perfectly clear?" I screamed, sticking my face directly in his face, daring him to make a move towards me.

Realizing the situation was about to get out of control, Tom asked Terry to step into the den for a short conference. I overheard my husband explain to Terry that my threat was no idle one and that I had the means to carry out that threat. Tom also explained that he would fully support me in my attempts to jail Terry. After Tom's "come to Jesus" meeting with Terry, things went smoothly and we got Mary Anne into treatment a week later. Again my husband had come to the rescue.

It was then that I began to appreciate Tom. Suddenly, he was someone I didn't know but liked nonetheless. This new Tom wasn't anything like the old Tom I married so many years ago. No longer irresponsible, Tom now took over and solved problems. Previously, my husband had been indifferent and sarcastic. After Mary Anne's near death experience, Tom emerged as a compassionate, involved family man. I still found it hard to release my tight control over my youngest daughter. Surprisingly, Tom didn't challenge me on that. Occasionally, he would suggest that I loosen the reigns over Katherine. But there were none of the bitter fights we used to have over her.

When Mary Anne came home from treatment listless and apathetic, it was Tom who came up with the perfect solution. Over breakfast, Tom asked if I still wanted to remodel the house.

"Of course, but it's not the time. Mary Anne's only been home less than seven days …"

"That's just the point," interrupted Tom. "She's been here a week and hasn't shown interest in anything so far. And what does our daughter love more than shopping for clothes?"

"Decorating," I said. "Oh, Tom, that's brilliant."

"And, you have my permission to go for broke, so to speak," Tom laughed.

At first, Mary Anne showed little interest in the process. But Tom helped peak her interest by peppering her with questions every evening after the news. He started by asking, "Mary Anne, what do you think of Pat's choice of decorators?"

This, of course, led my daughter into a lengthy discussion of the pros and cons of seeking professional help or doing it yourself. Mary Anne had done both with varying results. Next, my husband asked Mary Anne to explain what plans we had for the playroom and, more importantly, how we planned to change Tom's den, the same den he used to pay his bills and read his detective novels; in other words, the place Tom called his escape, his refuge, his favorite room. This resulted in a heated debate between Tom and Mary Anne. I marveled at how my daughter suddenly came alive. The old Mary Anne began to emerge, thanks to the insightfulness of my husband. As time passed, Mary Anne began to heal. When she left us at the end of the summer, my daughter seemed healthy in both body and spirit. But I knew what she was facing when she returned to New Orleans and that increased my fears for her. Again, Tom came to the rescue.

"Pat, you have to let go and have faith. We've done everything we can."

"I know, but is it enough?" I asked.

"Yes, it is," he said.

The day my second daughter left for New Orleans, I didn't think I could stand it. Terry had come to Lancaster to take her back to their home in New Orleans. As she stood in our driveway, her bags in the trunk of Terry's car, I reached out and hugged Mary Anne. As my daughter clung to me, we both began to sob. Once more Tom took control by pulling us apart and giving Mary Anne a big hug and saying, "Baby, it's time to go. Call us when you get home so we'll know you got there safely. And don't forget to call your Mama at least once a week."

Mary Anne nodded and said, "Okay, Daddy. I promise."

I stood there watching their car as they pulled out of the driveway. I continued to watch until they disappeared over the horizon. When I started to cry again, Tom put his arms around me and said, "Mary Anne knows we love her and she knows where to go and who to call if she needs help."

"But will she, Tom? Will she call if she needs us?"

"Of course she will," he assured me. "Hasn't she always?"

Tom was right. My middle daughter always came running home when things got tough, but that was before Terry.

Despite my fears, Tom's calming influence and unfaltering support did help. I began to rely more and more on his advice. And I shocked even myself by sharing my most serious concerns and deepest fears with Tom. To my surprise, he didn't belittle me or turn sarcastic. He was so unlike his former self; I finally asked what caused the change in him. His response caught me off guard.

"I've lost a daughter and almost lost another. I didn't want to lose anything or anyone else. Pat, I realized nothing was more important than my family. I also realized I could lose everything if I didn't change, really change."

"Well, you've certainly done that. You're not the man I married," I exclaimed.

"Is that a bad thing?" he asked.

I leaned over and kissed Tom on the cheek and said, "No, it's a good thing."

Tom surprised me by saying I had changed too – that despite my fears, I was not going off half-cocked and alienating everyone.

"The hard edges are beginning to smooth out," he joked.

"Maybe I've taken a page out of your book," I replied.

Chapter Fifteen
SEPTEMBER 1, 1964

I didn't see David until autumn. It happened a week before I started my freshman year at Belhaven. He had gone to Rush at Ole Miss and was home for the weekend. Mama was very proud of her first effort to renovate our eighty-year old home and equally eager to show off the results. An opportunity for just that presented itself during our Thursday night out at Angie's. Since Angie's was a popular Lancaster restaurant, it wasn't surprising that we would see the Bhaer family sitting one table away from us. During dinner, Daddy invited them home "to see what Pat's done with the house." The invitation was readily accepted. During the drive home, I alternated between excitement over seeing David again and stomach-churning nervousness.

The exterior of our home consisted of a large porch supported by wide columns and a new sunroof-carport protruding from the south side of the two- story wooden house. To the north was a fenced-in area, the residence of the family pet, Gordon, an exuberant hundred-pound yellow lab that had yet to meet a stranger. The minute Gordon heard the cars pulling in the driveway, he began to jump in place and bark in anticipation. David went straight to Gordon and gave him a gentle rub. Gordon responded with an appreciative lick on David's hand. The two were old friends, and it made me smile to see them together again.

The dining room was decorated in softly muted blues and greens. A large crystal chandelier hung above an ornately carved oblong mahogany table and chairs, which easily seated twelve or more. The dining room also contained a china cabinet, a large silver chest, and a Queen Anne sideboard. The windows were draped with cream-colored silk curtains.

In the center of the living room, a blue raised brocade sofa, fronted by a low marble-topped table, faced the fireplace on the left wall. Against the right wall was a large hutch containing cut-glass bowls and vases of various sizes and shapes. In the left-hand corner, sandwiched between two chairs of rose velvet, stood a round oak table with mother-of-pearl inlay. Other antique chairs were strategically placed about the room.

A long hallway led from the living room to the family room with several bedrooms in between. Near the end of the hallway was a curved staircase leading to the second story. The master bedroom and the twins' room were located on the first floor. Additionally, a small library was nestled next to the master bedroom and a breakfast area adjoined the kitchen. The second floor contained my room and Lisa's room, which had been turned into a guest room occupied by Mary Anne during her frequent visits.

Mama gave the Bhaers a brief tour of the house. Afterwards, the two families retreated to the playroom, except for me and David. We headed for my room. Different from its previous incarnation, my room was no longer pink but decorated in pale yellow and ocean blue. The spread covering my queen-sized bed had a yellow background decorated with blue sea-shells and starfish. The honey-colored wooden floors were covered with blue throw-rugs, and the walls were dotted with pictures of lighthouses and sailboats on an open sea. When we got to my room, I tried to fill the silence with conversation.

"How's school?"

"School hasn't really started, but I'm settling in, doing the frat thing."

"Are you going to pledge SAE?" I asked, hoping somehow to connect.

"Probably," responded David, his answers short and to the point.

I continued to probe, feeling awkward and inept. As I leaned over to turn on the record player, David grabbed me by the shoulders and pulled me toward him. We kissed, it seemed like, for several minutes. Suddenly, David pushed me away.

"Katie, I can't do this!"

David turned and left as quickly as he came. The record player was still on, and Ricky Nelson's "It's Up to You" filled the room.

In the months ahead, I played that scene over and over again in my head. I questioned myself constantly. What could I have done differently? What could I have said to make him stay? What could I have done to bring David back to me? The beginning of my college years should have been happy and exciting. I was young and my life was just beginning. But I felt so lonely. My days were filled with an ache, a longing for David, for the mere sight of him.

I wandered the Belhaven campus like a ghost, not really connecting with anyone or anything. I turned down numerous dates claiming that I had a boyfriend attending a college out of state. I went home every weekend and refused to attend any of the ballgames, dances or any student activities most college students enjoy. Finally, my roommate convinced me to make friends and participate in campus events by the beginning of my sophomore year. But I still refused to go out on a date, always hoping David would come back to me.

It would be almost two years before I would see David again. It was at Ray's funeral. Like his friend from Morganfield, Kentucky, Ray stepped on a land mine and pieces of him were sent home in a body bag for a military funeral. I alternated between gut-wrenching grief and red-hot anger at Ray for going to Vietnam in the first place. But deep down I knew he was lost to himself and everyone else the night Lisa's car hit a wet spot in the middle of the road.

It was at Ray's wake that I noticed David. I was sitting with Ray's cousin when I saw David standing in the doorway. We met in the center of the room. David hugged me and said the appropriate things, showed the right amount of concern and empathy, but there was a distant look in his eyes, a detachment that hadn't been there before. It was finally over and there was nothing I could do or say to change things. In an instant, I realized the difference and finally accepted the unacceptable.

After the memorial service, I went straight home. Lying on my bedside table was a letter from Ray, the last letter I would ever receive from him.

Dear Katie:

>*I probably should tear this letter up and not subject you to any more late-night terrors. I know I probably won't make it through this war and it is a war, even if the President and Congress call it a military conflict. I don't matter. As you know, I lost everything the night I lost your sister. But there are boys here that deserve a chance to live their lives and they will never get that chance. Katie, the war is already lost. We keep taking the same ground over and over again. I'm not a military expert, but you can't fight a defensive war and expect to win it. And then there are the people of Vietnam. The peasants, after years of abuse by the Saigon government, often side with the Viet Cong, who are relentless and determined. Many civilians support them. Ten-year olds wrapped in explosives are not uncommon. They think nothing of blowing themselves up, if they can blow you up as well. It's funny how war strips away the veneer of civilization. It makes you realize how little difference there is between us and our ancient ancestors. I'll never get used to the killing. The death of my friends, who had so many plans for their futures, and the killing I've done myself haunts my days and nights, and Johnson keeps sending more boys to die. Katie, I know these letters are a burden to you, but I want you to know the truth so you can tell others what's really going on over here.*

>*Take care of yourself, sweet girl, and don't forget me.*

Always, Ray

I lay in my bed, darkness enveloping me. I was too numb to cry and too troubled to sleep. My only hope was that Lisa was there waiting for Ray after he took that wrong step and was blown away in a flash of light.

Years later, I asked myself why – why did Ray have to die? Why did he give up on life so young? And why did he die in a jungle so far from home? But, more importantly, I wondered why those friends of Ray's with so many plans for the future had to die over something called "the domino theory"? Despite the effect of Ray's letters, I never participated in any anti-war demonstrations or even spoke out publicly against the war. I always thought there would be numerous opportunities to do so, and that I had plenty of time to pick and choose. I was wrong!

Chapter Sixteen
JUNE 6, 1968

After Ray's funeral, I went back to Belhaven College with the intention of putting David and the accompanying memories behind me. I met Jeffery in English Lit 201. It wasn't love at first sight, but instant "like." Jeffery had just broken up with Ann, a girl he had dated for six years. They dated throughout most of high school and the first two years at Belhaven. She had been a comfortable companion, but not the one to marry. Jeffery later told me that by his sophomore year he had decided to break up with her when she started talking marriage. I later learned that Jeffery strung Ann along until he met me, one of many disagreeable facts that I discovered about him. He may have broken up with Ann, but that didn't mean Jeffery wasn't the marrying kind. He proposed after one month of dating me, and I said "maybe."

My future husband asked me out three times before I finally agreed to go out with him on our first date. Jeffery took me to dinner at the King Edward Hotel and afterwards we danced on the roof-top. I knew he was trying hard to impress me, but I couldn't overcome the emptiness I felt over losing David. For the next four months, he laid on the charm, tried to be funny, and even offered to help me with my lit class. I know I seemed distant, even cold at times. Finally, I began to open up to Jeffery and talk about David. Once I started talking about him, I couldn't stop. Years later, my husband revealed how he resented being treated like my new best friend and not a love interest. It really pissed him off, he said, but I didn't know it at the time. Jeffery was good at holding things in. As a boy, he learned to restrain a lot of anger and disappointment, another ugly fact I would later learn about the man I married.

Jeffery looked nothing like David. His blonde hair and piercing blue eyes contrasted with David's brown hair and dark eyes. The only thing they had in common was their six-foot frames. Jeffery's good looks seemed to affect everyone but Jeffery. When I commented on how my friends drooled over him, he blushed and changed the subject. His seeming lack of ego, along with his sense of humor, friendliness, and self-confidence drew me to him. Jeffery also provided me with a warm sense of security, a safety net, so to speak. There was none of the stomach-churning range of emotions that David evoked. No roller-coaster ride, just a calm assurance that Jeffery loved me and would never abandon me.

The longer we dated, the more determined Jeffery was to marry me. Later, I discovered it had become a matter of pride to win me away from "my precious David."

When we were dating, he put on a good show. During his first weekend with my parents, he brought my mother flowers and Daddy a rare port wine, which he didn't drink. After we married, I discovered it was all an act; he hated my family. I never forgot the day I discovered his true feelings. It was one of those fall football weekends at Ole Miss. Like everyone else, we tailgated in the Grove with my family and some of their close friends. Daddy's former fraternity brothers and their wives joined us for roasted chicken and deviled eggs. Jeffery had too much to drink and let loose with his opinions once we got back to our tiny apartment.

As he was changing into some sweats, he told me what he really thought of me and my family. As he unbuttoned his shirt and flung it on the bed, Jeffery said, "It's amazing how your family thinks their genes are superior to everyone who doesn't have their superior pedigree."

"That's not true, Jeffery!"

"Yes, it is," he laughed. "You father is the only drunk I know that has the audacity to think he's better than everyone. He's just lucky, that's all. If he had come from my background, your precious father would be lying in a gutter right now."

My own voice rising, I pointed out that Daddy hadn't had a drink in years and that I regretted sharing Daddy's past with him. That added fuel to the fire and Jeffery began to tear into me.

"And, my dear wife, where did you get your ridiculous views? From that drunken father of yours? Certainly not from your bitchy mother."

"That's enough, Jeffery!" I screamed loudly.

"Do you know how many times I have had to bite my tongue," he continued, "just to keep from saying how stupid and naïve your ideas were? It irks me that you're allowed to go to the polls and cast your vote for some knee-jerk liberal. I pretended you had some sense and kept my mouth shut, but no more!" he roared.

None of his venom surfaced before we married. He played the role of devoted suitor superbly. We dated through the rest of college and each Christmas he proposed and every time I said "maybe". After graduation, Jeffery's proposals became more urgent. He was about to start law school and he wanted me with him. I said yes and planned the wedding for late August, since Jeffery was starting law school in early September.

What I didn't realize or know was Jeffery wanted someone to cook his meals, iron his shirts, and provide a clean room for his studies. Additionally, he wouldn't have to bother with the courting process or making that three hour drive to Lancaster every weekend. He didn't tell me any of this. He simply said he loved me and didn't want to be separated from me. The truth was far more damning. Besides wanting me as "chief cook and bottle washer," Jeffery, in one of his more vicious moments, told me my pedigree had a lot to do with why he married me.

"It's true, my love, that you playing hard to get was a turn-on, but the real turn-on was the prominence of your decadent family. If people only knew how screwed up they are," he said, laughing in his nasty little way.

I glared at him as he continued.

"Old money goes a long way in climbing the corporate ladder, and I intend to have a wife with a pedigree helping me climb that ladder.

None of this was evident before we married, when he told me he wanted the wedding to take place before he left for law school. His pleading and insistent behavior had its desired effect. It led to a flurry of activity. Mama, Mary Anne, and I literally shopped until we dropped from exhaustion. After a particularly difficult day, which included picking out silverware and china, I headed for the playroom, turned on the TV, and sank into the nearest chair. The breaking news hit me like a thunderbolt. Bobby was dead. Mama's timing couldn't have been worse. She took one look at the TV and then, dripping with her customary venom, declared, "Well, I guess there won't be another Kennedy in the White House, will there, Katherine?"

If looks could kill, then Mama would have been dead in an instant. It would be years before I fully realized what we had lost with the deaths of Dr. King and Bobby Kennedy. But in 1968, I was just too angry and disgusted to feel or understand anything other than an overwhelming urge to slap Mama the way she used to slap me.

Mama had already infuriated me when she questioned me about my pending marriage and my feelings for Jeffery. We were picking out china at Fred's store when she brought up the subject for the tenth time.

"Katherine, are you sure about this marriage? What do you really know about Jeffery?"

"Mama, I know him, okay? We've dated for almost two years!"

"But what do you know about his background, his family?" Mama questioned.

"How many times do I have to tell you?" I yelled. "His parents died when Jeffery was eight," I answered, picking up a plate and examining it.

Not willing to let it go, she pushed on. "Is that all he told you about them?"

"No, he said his father was a truck driver and his mother was a waitress. Mama, how much could an eight-year old remember?"

"What about aunts, the uncle that raised him, his grandparents? What about his other relatives in Tannersville?

That's where he's from, right?" Mama asked, dripping with sarcasm. Jeffery grew up in a town of five thousand, sixty miles south of Jackson, where everyone knew everyone.

"You know darn well it is, and why the third degree?" I asked, getting irritated by all the questions.

"Because his explanations are so pat, so smooth, so perfect; too perfect. I'm sorry. I just don't trust him, Katherine. Believe me, I know the type," she responded, Mama's voice rising several octaves as she tried to convince me that I was making a mistake.

"I think we need to change the subject. What about this pattern for everyday?"

"Katherine, please listen to me," Mama insisted. "I don't want you to make the same mistake others in this family have made . . ."

"You really don't like him do you?" I yelled, interrupting her.

"It's not a matter of liking or disliking him. I just wish I knew more about Jeffery and wish you knew more about him, that's all."

"Mama, I know enough. He loves me and he'll never leave me," I said, suddenly looking away from her.

"Is this about David? You're still in love with him, aren't you?" she whispered, not wanting anyone to hear, especially Mr. Bhaer.

I crossed the room to look at the crystal. Mama followed me. At that point, Mary Anne entered the store. Looking over my shoulder, I inquired in a loud voice, loud enough for everyone in the store to hear. "Is that what Mary Anne told you?"

"No, Katherine, it's what I know! No one has to tell me that you still love David. Sweetheart, please don't marry a man you don't love!"

Obviously moved by Mama's endearment, I looked her in the eye and said softly, "Mama, David and I are over, and I care deeply for Jeffery…"

"But, you don't love him," she interrupted, attempting to make me see reason. At that point, I bristled and threatened to leave if Mama didn't change the subject.

Three days before the wedding, Mama begged me to reconsider my decision to marry. Again, I gave her a steely-eyed look and said I was going to marry Jeffery and that was the end of that. The night before I married, I found a letter from Mama on my bedside table.

Katherine,

> *When you told me about your engagement, I felt a cold chill. My mother married the wrong man, and it ended horribly. I don't want you to make the same mistake. I pray your marriage won't end badly. Look at your sister's marriage – drugs and near death!*
>
> *My Katherine, you are so willful, so bright. You have so much potential. I don't want all of that destroyed by a difficult situation. I know you are a grown woman, and I can no longer protect you, but please think about what I have said.*

Mama

The next day I married Jeffery.

Later, much later, I overheard a conversation between Jeffery and his Uncle Billy. I learned that my husband's parents had not died in a car wreck when he was only eight years old. His father died during Jeffery's junior year at Belhaven. He admitted to me that he didn't even go home for the funeral. When his mother passed away the following year, he celebrated with his buddies by getting drunk.

Everything he told me about his parents was a lie. When I confronted him about it, more nasty truths came out.

"Why did you lie to me?" I asked.

"Because my father was the town drunk. Everybody knew it. He would come home after a long haul, get drunk, and beat Mama and me. Mama wasn't much better. She probably slept with every male in Tannersville above the age of eighteen."

"Jeffery, how awful!"

"In elementary school, other boys would call Mama dirty names and I would fight them. Most of the time, I would whip their asses. Every other day, I would end up in the Principal's office, and every week Daddy would take a belt to me. As I grew older, dear wife, I learned to pretend it didn't bother me, that I didn't care if my Mama was a whore. But I did care! I studied hard so I could get away from Daddy and that white trash slut. I left Tannersville after high school and never looked back. So now you know."

"Why didn't you tell me the truth? Didn't you realize I would understand, or try to?" I asked.

"I don't want to talk about it, and you better not tell that snotty family of yours," he screamed.

The truth about Jeffery's mother and father wasn't the only secret he kept to himself. While we were dating, Jeffery lived in fear that his former girlfriend would reveal part of his past. But we didn't run in the same circles. Besides, Ann only knew bits and pieces of Jeffery's previous life. She was from Hattiesburg, a town forty miles south of Tannersville. He certainly covered his tracks well. He never took Ann to his hometown to meet his parents. Covering his tracks was a habit that seemed to serve Jeffery well as he grew older and more successful.

Throughout our marriage, I would find out more, much more. If only I had listened to Mama.

Chapter Seventeen
AUGUST 25, 1968

Despite the fact that things were improving between Tom and me, and Mary Anne seemed happy, all was not well. My middle daughter called me at least twice a week and let me know she was doing okay. I considered the fact that Terry was traveling a lot and not home to influence my daughter a good thing.

My most immediate and pressing concern was my youngest, Katherine. Her engagement to Jeffery, a boy she met her second year at Belhaven, alarmed me. The minute I met him I knew he was a fake. If Katherine wasn't still in love with David and on the rebound, she would have seen it for herself. I tried to point out that Jeffery's past wasn't an open book. Whenever I questioned him about his family, the answers he gave were far too smooth, too pat. He never really answered my questions. Whenever the questions got too probing, Jeffery managed to change the subject. Usually, his response consisted of insincere compliments and overblown attempts to ingratiate himself with me and my husband.

When Katherine and David broke up, I was relieved. I didn't want her to learn about the affair with Fred. Later, I realized how devastated my daughter was over the breakup, and I began to fear for her. I shared this with Tom. We were sitting in the backyard drinking lemonade and watching the sun go down, when I mentioned, "Tom, I'm concerned about Katherine. She's stopped going outside the house. It's her senior year, and she should be going to football games, dances, senior parties ..."

"I know. I know. Give her time."

"Time for what?" I asked, impatient with Tom's response.

"Pat, Katie is hurting. She doesn't want to run into David, and there's the shame she feels. He broke up with her, not the other way around."

"My Lord, you make it sound like some great love affair. She's a teenager, for God's sake!"

"That doesn't mean she doesn't love him, and you're going to have to accept that. It's not something you can dismiss as puppy love."

"You mean she's not going to get over this anytime soon?"

"That's right."

As I got up to go inside, I said, "You know at first, I was glad. She was staying close to home so nothing bad could happen to her. But now, I'm worried, really worried."

"Give it time, Pat," said Tom with a sigh. "Give it time."

When Katherine first told me she was seeing someone, I was happy. I felt she was finally moving on and letting go of her past with David. Then I met Jeffery. When happiness turned to bone-chilling fear, I consulted Tom. He agreed there was reason for alarm. He didn't trust Jeffery any more than I did. Terry took an instant dislike to my daughter's fiancé. Obviously, the schemer recognized someone similar to himself.

When I tried to reason with Katherine, she refused to listen. Angry at her refusal to see reason, I resorted to my old ways. I became sarcastic and judgmental about anything and everything important to my daughter, Kennedys included. The looks she gave me made me realize that, once again, I had gone too far. Late one afternoon, shortly after Tom had arrived home from work, he told me so.

"Pat, your heavy-handedness is only alienating Katherine."

"She won't listen," I explained as Tom turned on the evening news. "What am I supposed to do?" I asked. "I'm at my wits end. I can't ... I won't let her end up like my mother," I cried.

"What does your mother have to do with it?" asked Tom.

It was then that I told my husband the story of Grace. After he recovered from the initial shock, Tom said, "Now I understand. Your mother's story explains a lot. No wonder you're fearful for Katie. But baby, it still doesn't change anything. You can't put her under glass. Our daughter has to make her own mistakes. You've got to let go."

Tom was right but I didn't want to hear it. "Tom, I can't just give up, not yet."

"Then write her a letter, put it on her pillow the night before the wedding, and let her sleep on it."

I kissed him on the forehead, and before leaving the playroom, I said, "How did you get so smart in your old age?" I joked. "As usual, your solution is perfect. I just hope my words have some effect," I said.

"Baby, if your words have no effect, you'll have to let her make her own way," Tom warned. "Have faith! Pat, if things don't work out, our girl knows we're here for her," Tom reminded me.

Katherine ignored my advice and married Jeffery. After that, I did a lot of praying, a lot of worrying, and some letting go. Again, Tom's advice and support helped. My husband pointed out that his shoulders were for leaning on and that they were also drip-dry. I used those shoulders a lot and shed more than a few tears on them.

With thoughts of my youngest daughter getting married and the twins growing older, I considered getting a part-time job, as well as doing some volunteer work. My boys didn't need me as much as when they were toddlers, plus I needed to take my mind off of Katherine's not-so-wise decision to marry Jeffery.

As my daughter made it down the aisle in her simple but beautiful satin dress, beaded around the neck and wrists with a wide train, I tried to concentrate on my future and not on Katherine's.

At the reception afterwards, I brought up the subject with Tom of working part-time and volunteering around town. He readily agreed. "I think that's a wonderful idea. What about coming to work with me as my assistant?"

"Tom, I'm not so sure about that. Won't you get sick of me at your side during the day and then having to deal with me at home too?" I asked.

"I can't think of anything better," responded Tom. "Pat, you've worked at the bank before and you know its ins and outs as well as I do."

"Are you sure? My job was as a teller, not assistant to the president."

"Baby, we've been married more years than either of us can count, and how many times over those years have we talked about the bank? You're perfect for the job, believe me."

With that, he took me by the hand and said, "Let's join the others. It's getting time for Jeffery and Katherine to leave for their honeymoon."

As I watched my daughter and her new husband drive out of sight, I thought about the boy she loved and the one she married and hoped against hope everything would turn out okay.

The next week, I started my job as Tom's assistant. Everything went surprisingly well. It gave Tom and me even more to talk about and gave me welcome relief from my constant worry over Katherine, not to mention Mary Anne. I thought to myself, "Boy, can my daughters pick 'em!"

A month after I returned to work, my contentment with my new job, along with my security in my marriage, seemed to be seriously threatened when Chrissie breezed through the front door shortly after the bank opened for business. I managed to intercept her before she reached my husband's office.

"What do you want?" I asked.

"I thought I might open a savings account," she answered, looking around for Tom.

I responded to her obvious ploy to peak my husband's interest in her by blocking her path and saying, "There's a bank two blocks from here that I'm sure would love your business. Unfortunately for you, neither you nor your money is welcome here."

"Why don't we let Tom be the judge of that," responded Chrissie, trying to push her way past me.

By now, people were watching us, including Tom, who had just slipped out of his office. He quickly made his way to us, put his arm around my waist, and asked Chrissie, "And to what do we owe the pleasure?"

"I want to open a bank account, savings …"

"Wonderful," interrupted Tom. "Pat can help you with that," he said with a smile.

"Pat!" yelled Chrissie.

"Yes, Pat. She's my right hand, and I depend on her to handle everything I can't or don't want to deal with." Tom then turned and went back into his office, giving a back-handed wave.

With a smirk on my face, I asked Chrissie to step into my office.

"No, thank you!" she shouted and stomped out of our bank and our lives.

My life was evolving. The more I grew to depend on Tom, the more I let go and let my children, especially Katherine, live their own lives. Some of the old insecurity, the fear that was my constant companion when I was young, began to subside. Tom noticed the change. After a time, a long time, we began to share a bed again. One night after love-making, when we were wrapped in each other's arms enjoying the after-glow, Tom commented on the change.

"Pat, you're not the same insecure girl I married."

"What do you mean?" I asked, snuggling under Tom's arm.

"You're more relaxed, less judgmental, more live and let live."

"It's about time, right?" I laughed.

"Yes, I guess so. What brought about this miraculous change?"

I looked into his eyes before answering him and saw something I thought I'd never see in my husband's eyes -- I saw love.

"You had a lot to do with it," I answered. "Tom, you've changed yourself. You've gone from being abusive to being a loving, supportive husband. I think I'm beginning to fall for you," I said with a laugh.

Tom reached over and kissed me and said, "The feeling is mutual."

At the time I didn't fully analyze the situation, but later I began to sort things out. I realized finally I had something I could trust, someone I could depend on. Tom was there for me and he wasn't going away. My husband still had his moments; "dry drunks" is what he called them. But those episodes occurred less and less. Tom grew into the man he always wanted to be. In response, I started to become the woman I wanted to be.

Through it all, the drinking, the betrayals, the death of Lisa, and the near death of Mary Anne, it was there – the seed, the capacity for something more than mutual contempt.

Chapter Eighteen
AUGUST 30, 1968

My wedding was very simple. I had one matron of honor, my sister, Mary Anne, and two bridesmaids, my Belhaven roommate and, of course, Betsy. Jeffery was relieved that the wedding was small, since he had no family to speak of and few friends who wanted to participate in the ceremony. The small chapel at St. Phillips was filled to capacity and decorated in the fall colors of yellow, burnt orange and deep red, which created an aura of autumn splendor, despite the fact that the August heat had reached well into the nineties with no relief in sight.

The pianist filled the church with the lovely strains of "Ave Maria" and other appropriate selections befitting a wedding ceremony. I was sequestered in a corner room waiting for my cue. I couldn't help but feel that Mozart's "Requiem Mass," the one that destroyed his health and sanity during its creation, would have been a more appropriate musical selection. I remember Mama begging me to reconsider my decision to marry Jeffery and Betsy reminding me that I still loved David. I denied it, but I knew she was right. The desire to break and run was almost overpowering; only the thought of hurting Jeffery prevented my panic from taking over. The concerned look on Mama's face almost reduced me to tears.

The entire ceremony was like an out-of-body experience. My body went through the motions while my mind looked on with utter detachment. Once the ceremony was completed, I relaxed somewhat and tried to enjoy the reception, pretending it was a party just like any other party, except now I was somebody's wife. That somebody, my husband, suddenly felt like a stranger. I longed for the comfort of home and familiar surroundings. I avoided Mama's presence, for I knew I would lose control and weep helplessly in Mama's arms if I allowed myself to feel the grief I was trying so hard to suppress.

The four-hour drive to New Orleans was spent in silence. The havoc I felt, coupled with the beginnings of a severe head cold, prevented any extended conversations. Much to my relief, Jeffery, feeling drained himself, agreed to postpone sex. My last waking thoughts were not of the sleeping stranger snoring peacefully beside me but of David. Where was he at that exact moment? What was he doing and did he ever think of me?

During one of our many fights, Jeffery revealed that I called out David's name in my sleep that first night of our honeymoon. He said if he had been like his father, he would have knocked me out of the bed. He said I was a lucky bitch. He revealed that calling out David's name was the real reason he avoided sex with me the entire weekend.

The days that followed weren't so bad. It was easy to pretend we were just good friends vacationing together. After all, Jeffery was smart and witty, which meant he was generally good company. The drive back home was pleasant enough and then there was the move to Oxford. The unpacking and settling into the married couples' dorm kept me pretty busy. I began to think of Jeffery as a glorified roommate, and somehow this pretense lessened the sting of disappointment, the heartache of what might have been if Jeffery had been someone other than himself. I threw myself into decorating our new home, which consisted of a bedroom, bathroom, and combination kitchen and living room area.

As weeks stretched into months, I established a routine of housekeeping and socializing with other law school wives. The familiarity of my everyday tasks, coupled with a determination to make the marriage work, helped me to bury my disappointment. But it didn't rid me of the numbness I sometimes felt, or dispel the deep-seated depression that enveloped my psyche. So deep was this sadness that I didn't recognize it for what it was. Others, however, saw what was happening to me and were alarmed by the change. Only Jeffery, totally involved in his studies, was seemingly blind to what others could clearly see.

He spent most of his time with his study group. The only time we were together was breakfast and supper. Jeffery seemed happy that I made no real demands on his time or attention, since all of his energies were spent on his studies. Jeffery said other men in his class complained that their wives wanted sex and nights together. He was gratified that I never did. I think we both knew the reason why.

As time passed, some of the depression lifted. Instead I became bored and restless. I wanted to teach. It led to my first big fight with Jeffery. It was in the middle of dinner when I broached the subject. When I mentioned my intention to start teaching, Jeffery slammed his fist on the table, almost breaking it.

"I'll be damned if my wife is going to work for a living. In case you don't know, I don't believe in that women's lib shit."

"Jeffery, I was trained to teach. Why go to school if I can't use my education?" I reasoned.

"To find a husband, and this husband doesn't want a working wife. I don't give a damn how many bra-burning bull dykes scream for liberation, you're not working! It's time you started acting right and learned your place, just like those agitating niggers."

"Don't start that, Jeffery!" I screamed, which seemed to fuel his rage.

"Yeah, somebody needs to put them in their place."

What I didn't know at the time was his Uncle Billy had been trying to put the "coloreds," as he put it, in their place since he was a teenager. Good ole Uncle Billy belonged to the Klan and Jeffery idolized him. Billy had taught my husband to hunt and fish and, most of all, to hate.

I looked at the veins standing out in his neck and changed the subject. But my restlessness grew worse and so did my resentment.

I had always been good at avoiding sex with my glorified roommate. Now I no longer pretended I had an upset stomach or a serious headache. As time passed, Jeffery became bitter and more verbally abusive. Whatever I felt, believed, or thought was the opposite of what he felt, believed, or thought. We fought over Vietnam, civil rights, gun control and, most of all, equal rights for women. The more I refused his advances, the more demeaning he became. Finally, I couldn't take it anymore and asked for a divorce. It was near the end of law school. Early one afternoon, he came home from Administrative Law class and found me packing.

"What the hell do you think you're doing?" Jeffery screamed.

"What does it look like?" I screamed back.

"You're not leaving me."

"Jeffery, what's the point?" I shot back. "We're barely civil to each other. You know it's over. Please let me go," I pleaded.

"No. You're not going to humiliate me. You don't have cause and I'm not going to give you cause."

"What's humiliating about realizing it's over for us?"

Suddenly Jeffery started laughing, a sharp, unpleasant sound that grated on my nerves. "That's rich! There has to be something there for it to be over." Jeffery grabbed me by the shoulders and shook me. "Don't you know I've known from the very beginning that you were thinking of your precious David? Do you really think I was fooled by your endless headaches and stomachaches?"

"Then why, why won't you let me go?"

He leaned into me and said, "Remember our vows; for better or worse. You don't leave me. I leave you - when I'm ready." That was his parting shot before slamming the front door and screeching out of the driveway. At that moment, I thought of my parents and how life repeats itself. He came home late that night, obviously drunk. After that, we maintained separate bedrooms and only pretended to be in love. I knew Jeffery was finding comfort elsewhere, but I didn't care, as long as he left me alone.

After Jeffery refused to let me go, thoughts of David crept into my mind more often than I would have liked. I tried to push him from my thoughts, but I couldn't. Some days those thoughts were constant. I knew my parents were still good friends with the Bhaers, so I wasn't surprised when I overheard Daddy telling Mama that David had enlisted in the Air Force.

They were in the den and it was late afternoon when I heard Daddy say, "Fred says David will start his training in two weeks."

"I hope to God he won't end up in Vietnam," exclaimed Mama.

"Really," said Daddy with a sigh.

"Tom, how long will he be…?"

"Be away?" interjected Daddy.

"Yes, how long?"

"At least four years, maybe longer."

As I listened, I knew what my parents were thinking. The next day, I went shopping with Mama, specifically to find an outfit for Jeffery's graduation. In the middle of trying on a navy blue dress with a scooped-out neck, I told Mama I knew David was about to start his flight training.

I continued by making the unspoken but obvious observation, "So it's not likely I will run into him anytime soon."

"No, honey, that's not likely," answered Mama as she pulled several dresses from the rack.

"And I guess I should put him out of my mind," I said.

"Yes, if you want any peace."

"I know, Mama, I know."

With that, I dropped the subject, but I still thought of David often. It was those thoughts that made my existence with Jeffery tolerable but bittersweet.

After law school, Jeffery became an associate in a Jackson firm specializing in corporate law. Being in Jackson made our pretense more bearable. There were more distractions, plus the nearness of family. Refuge was only forty miles away. I even began to entertain, which pleased Jeffery. He said I was an excellent hostess. Jeffery considered that a true asset on his climb up the corporate ladder.

Chapter Nineteen
MAY 12, 1972

The move to Jackson proved to be a positive distraction for me. In addition to the nearness of family, there was my work as a substitute teacher. Jeffrey didn't consider substituting a real job since other wives in the firm were doing the same thing. It was what you did until your husband received his promotion or won his first big case. Only then could a wife start the process of baby-making, her real job.

I met Ruthie on the first day I substituted at St. Anthony's. She was beautiful, with skin the color of milk chocolate and large brown eyes that accented her small face. We became instant friends. Her husband was stationed in Japan, so Ruthie remained in Mississippi and taught school. She was living with her in-laws until Max completed his tour of duty the end of the following year. We ate lunch together and then shopped for shoes. After school, I went to Ruthie's house and drank Sangrias. We became so close that I failed to notice the stares from strangers when we ate out together or shopped together. But Ruthie noticed. It was the first thing Southern blacks learned to do - notice things. Ruthie and I talked about almost everything. I soon realized I had no concept of what it was like to be black in Mississippi or what the movement hoped to accomplish. Thanks to Ruthie, I became more aware. I also realized that there was a part of Ruthie that was off limits to everyone but her own kind. Even our friendship couldn't breach that divide. As time passed, I began to understand why it had to be that way. I also understood that this divide wouldn't go away quickly. But none of this cooled my admiration for my new friend or prevented me from spending time with her.

What I failed to realize was that in the spring of 1972, Mississippi wasn't that far away from the violence and resistance of the 1960's. Too many people noticed our friendship and too many people resented us for it. Things were building, and it led to one more confrontation with Jeffery. The intensity of that confrontation didn't surprise me. What did surprise me were the things I learned about my husband that I hadn't realized prior to that balmy day in April. By the time we moved to Jackson, I knew Jeffery was a bigot, but I didn't know the depth of his contempt for those he considered inferior. He was such an actor that he managed to conceal his true self through the years of our courtship and early marriage.

It all started with an uneventful school day and seemingly innocent invitation. I asked Ruthie to my home for an after-school Sangria. Jeffrey was out of town and wasn't expected back for several days - or at least that's what I had been told.

We had just settled in the den, Sangrias in hand, when the door burst open. There stood Jeffery, red-faced. His mouth formed a perfect snarl. His voice sounded guttural. At first I couldn't understand him. Then his words became perfectly clear. The hatred spewed out of him.

"What the fuck is going on here?" he bellowed.

"What does it look like?"

"It looks like the idiot brought home a nigger, and you better get that black bitch out of here now!" he screamed.

Ruthie had already crossed the room and was on her way out when I tried to stop her. I reached out and touched her arm and said, "I'm so sorry." Her face registered pain and resignation, and then she was gone without a word. I spun around and slapped Jeffery so hard it left an imprint of my hand on his face. He grabbed me by both shoulders and shook me. He leaned into my face, so close I could smell his breath and whispered.

"If you ever bring that bitch to our home again, I won't be responsible for what I'll do."

I whispered back, "I hate you!"

He laughed and left the room.

I later learned that one of the teachers at St. Anthony's had alerted Jeffery about my planned get-together with Ruthie. It seems her husband and mine had joined the law firm at the same time. Jeffery even tried to get my mother involved in his plan to end my friendship with Ruthie. Mama, to her credit and to my surprise, refused.

Jeffery need not have worried. My friendship with Ruthie ended that balmy day in April, the day of the confrontation. I tried to apologize – to make amends, but nothing worked. Ruthie quietly accepted my apologies and excuses and then made excuses of her own. Every invitation was politely rejected. She always had something else to do, some other obligation. We spoke to each other in the halls and the teacher's lounge, but the animated talks of two friends were gone, along with the private jokes, the gossip, and the shared secrets. It saddened me. I felt a void, but I understood. Why would Ruthie want to be friends with someone who was married to a man like Jeffery? It was wrong of me to be such a coward, to wait until my husband was supposed to be out of town and then secretly invite Ruthie to my home. Why hadn't I left Jeffery after law school? I had asked myself that question on numerous occasions, so had my mother and my sister, Mary Anne. The answer was always the same. I wasn't ready. Looking back, I think it was fear: fear of starting over, fear of being alone, fear of the unknown, and fear of never finding what I had with David. Jeffery was familiar; I had financial security and knew what to expect. I continued with my marriage through the fear and shame and finally the return of a familiar numbness.

I settled into the role of hostess to Jeffery's partners and fellow associates in his law firm. At least twice a month, Jeffery and I would host a dinner party or cook-out for various members of his firm, always making sure at least one partner was in attendance.

I would watch in amazement as my husband courted the upper echelon in his firm with much the same persistence and relentless determination he displayed when courting me. I alternated between amusement and disgust. After one of those parties, I commented on Jeffery's brown-nosing techniques as I cleared the plates from the dining room table.

"Jeffery, you never cease to amaze me. Do you ever tire of the unfaltering flattery or false charm? You should go into politics. You are so good at telling people exactly what they want to hear without ever hinting at what you really feel or think."

"Are you calling me a fake?" demanded Jeffery.

"Yes," I shouted back. "You are the ultimate fake. I doubt you've had an honest thought or feeling since childhood."

"What is this, Katherine? Another attempt at a divorce that you know won't happen?" he threatened.

"No, Jeffery," I said with a sigh. "It's just an observation."

"You want to know something ironic, dear wife?" he asked, dripping with sarcasm.

"What, Jeffery?" I responded, putting the last of the silverware in the dishwasher.

"Anne Hill. You know Frank's wife?"

"Yes, Frank, the senior partner's wife?" I interjected.

"Anne said she thought you and I were the perfect couple, not just because we give wonderful parties but it was obvious to her that we were crazy about each other."

"So I guess that makes me a fake, too," I said.

"Yes, I guess it does," said Jeffery with mocking laughter.

As I opened the door to my empty bedroom, I thought of Jeffery's laughter and shivered.

The next eruption in my daughter's life occurred over a friend she had made while substitute teaching. Her friend was black and, of course, Jeffery didn't approve. I had long since stopped trying to influence my daughter's views, much less her actions. My husband had convinced me that it was not only futile but aggravating for all concerned. Times were changing, and I had made peace with the fact that my children's opinions, beliefs, etc. weren't the same as mine, and that, in the long run, that was okay.

We had so many debates over that one issue. Sometimes those debates were angry, almost violent in nature. But I mellowed with time and began to realize that many of my attitudes were based on fear and lots of insecurity.

When the Civil Rights Movement was in its infancy and Katherine was a schoolgirl, I was afraid of what people would do if they knew what my outspoken daughter actually thought. How would her opinions affect Tom's business? What would my friends and neighbors think of me?

When I married Tom, I felt woefully inadequate as a wife and hostess. Tom came from a very old and very prominent southern family. I felt everyone was watching me, judging me. One false step and I would be ostracized and Tom would be pitied. As I grew older and my marriage stabilized, I realized those fears were unfounded. But fears about social condemnation when it came to civil rights weren't unrealistic. People who were brave enough to support the Movement usually paid some sort of price. I wasn't that brave and told Tom just that.

It was shortly after Martin Luther King's "I Have a Dream" speech. My daughter went on and on about it, and I raised the issue with Tom by saying, "Don't you realize we could be shunned by our neighbors and friends if Katherine goes too far; not to mention what will happen to the bank!" I screeched.

"Pat, for God's sake, who's going to pay any attention to a schoolgirl? You've got to get a grip!"

"You're the one that needs to get a grip! We live in a society that doesn't like renegades, and that's what your daughter is with her outlandish talk!"

My warnings led to another fight with no change in Tom's attitude or Katherine's behavior. I lived in fear for a long time. Unfortunately, that fear fueled my former rage. Thankfully, I had long since put that behind me and my children's views were no longer threatening to me.

It was a beautiful spring day, and I had just finished cleaning out the hall closet and was ready to tackle the bedroom, which involved an over-stuffed roll-topped chest, when the phone rang. It was Jeffery, irate as usual about Katherine.

"Pat, your daughter's done it again. She's going to ruin my chances to make partner in the firm. You've got to straighten her out!" he pleaded.

"Jeffery, what are you talking about?" I asked, slightly irritated that my son-in-law had spoiled a perfectly good day.

"Your daughter's new nigger friend. That's what I'm talking about…"

"I still don't know what you're talking about. Be specific and cut the dramatics," I said, interrupting his rant, wishing he would get on with it. I could never completely hide my feelings, and I'm sure Jeffery knew exactly how I felt about him.

"Your daughter made friends with a nigger while substitute teaching and brought the bitch home for drinks – my home, dammit!" said Jeffery, his voice rising as he became more agitated.

"I thought it was Katherine's home, too," I said, knowing my observation would anger him.

"I still call the shots, and I don't want any niggers in my house!" he said, becoming increasingly loud.

"First of all," I said, "I don't know why you're telling me any of this. Secondly, I don't tell my daughter who to socialize with."

I went on to tell him that my daughter had a mind of her own, and if he didn't like it, he should cut his losses. At that point, Jeffery asked me what I meant by that remark. Finally losing my temper and patience, I told him he knew exactly what I meant and slammed down the phone. I was still mad when Katherine called several hours later.

"Mama, I'm sorry," she said.

"Don't apologize. You're not the one that made me mad."

"I appreciate what you told Jeffery – I mean the part about me having a mind of my own."

"Well, you do, don't you?" I laughed. "What are you going to do about your friend?"

"Nothing. I've lost Ruthie as a friend, thanks to Jeffery."

The next day I brought up the subject again. I invited Katherine for lunch and while putting away the chicken salad and strawberries, I mentioned my daughter's lost friendship.

"Why don't you make another attempt to talk to Ruthie?"

"Mama, I've tried but it's no use. She's polite but not interested in being friends with me, and I don't blame her. Who wants to be friends with the wife of a raging bigot?"

"You know, I'm not the most liberal person when it comes to race, but I hate to see Jeffery control your life and who you associate with. Honey, you never let me dictate what you did or didn't do. Why do you let Jeffery?" I asked.

"Mama, the damage can't be undone, not with Ruthie. But you need to know I do fight back. I really do. I'm just not ready to broach the subject of divorce again, not yet."

"Why not? When are you going to leave him? You're obviously miserable. I don't know why…"

"Mama, please," pleaded Katherine.

"Okay, okay. I'll mind my own business," I said with a sigh.

Several hours later, Mary Anne's crisis with Terry pushed Katherine and her problems with Jeffery to the back of my mind. Tom was again very supportive and, surprisingly, so was Jeffery. Things rocked along, but I knew it wasn't over. Sooner or later, the facade Jeffery and Katherine called a marriage would come crashing down. I just hoped my daughter wouldn't be hurt by the fallout.

My own mistakes and my mother's tragic, misspent life came rushing back. They flooded my thoughts every time I looked at my middle daughter. I prayed that God would spare Katherine the heartache I believed was in her future. There was her marriage and the boy that she still loved, the son of Fred and all that entailed.

Chapter Twenty One
AUGUST 1, 1974

The years passed quickly and there were many changes in my family. The twins were growing up. Both played Little League and golf and entered every tennis tournament within a 300-mile radius.

I enjoyed watching them grow. What I didn't enjoy watching was the continuing drama of Mary Anne and Terry's descent into drugs. After Mary Anne's near death experience and subsequent treatment for alcohol and drug abuse, she did well for about a year. My sister continued with her out-patient treatment, and followed her 12-step program, as well as following a healthy program of diet and exercise. But that didn't stop Terry from trying to entice her with sleeping pills, pain pills and anti-anxiety medication. Finally, the temptation became too great, and she started using again. Terry, wanting someone to party with, was more than willing to supply my sister with all the drugs she could consume.

It all came to a head one August afternoon. Like everyone else, I was glued to the television watching the Watergate scandal play itself out. I was listening to Nixon give his "I'm not a crook" speech when the telephone rang.

It was Mama. I could hear the fear in her voice. "Well, Terry's really done it now," Mama exclaimed.

"Hello to you, too," I said.

"Katherine, I'm not in the mood. Terry's been arrested and your sister is hysterical and high on God knows what!"

"Mama, slow down and tell me exactly what happened."

"I'm not totally sure. I got a call from the police station in Hattiesburg from some sergeant who said they had stopped Terry

128

for going through a red light and they clocked him at eighty."

"Oh my God, he could have killed someone!"

"Yes, he could have killed your sister. Mary Anne was in the passenger seat!" exclaimed Mama, nearly hysterical herself.

"Mama, calm down and breathe," I cautioned. "What happened after they stopped Terry?" I asked.

"Well, the Sergeant said that Terry was slurring his words. So they gave him a field sobriety test and then took him to Forrest General and drew blood."

"Why did they do that?"

"According to the Sergeant, Terry had a seizure. Doctors at Forrest General said he was suffering from the effects of alcohol, cocaine, and morphine."

"How in the world did he get his hands on cocaine and morphine?" I asked, getting more apprehensive as Mama spoke.

"I don't know. Once they treated him and it was safe to release him, the police took him to the city jail. He hasn't been before a judge and Mary Anne said Terry won't go before a judge until tomorrow morning."

"What do you want me to do?" I asked.

"Call Jeffery. Tell him what's happened and see if he can find us a really good criminal lawyer in the Hattiesburg area."

"Okay."

"And can you ride with me to Hattiesburg? I need to pick up Mary Anne. She's still at the police station, and I'm too nervous to drive there by myself."

"Sure, I'll be waiting. By the time you get here, I should have the name of a good lawyer we can contact when we get down there."

After Mama arrived, she switched from the driver's seat to the passenger side. She handed me the keys and asked, "Katherine, will you drive? I just can't."

"Sure, Mama," I said, looking into her terrified eyes. "It's going to be okay," I assured her, but I wasn't convinced myself that everything was going to be okay.

"Katherine, what are we going to do? I could care less about Terry, but I'm afraid for Mary Anne. I don't think I could stand to lose another child," said Mama, her voice breaking and her eyes full of unspent tears.

"Mama, we'll do whatever we have to. We're not going to lose her, I promise," I said, wondering how in the world I could keep that promise.

When we got to the police station, Mary Anne was sitting on a wooden bench in the reception area. Her eyes were big as saucers, and she was shaking all over from fear. I don't believe I had ever seen her so frightened. She flew into Mama's arms, crying hysterically. The effects of whatever Terry had given Mary Anne had worn off, and she had all the characteristics of someone who had reached the end of her endurance.

I was shocked by her appearance. Her hair was limp and stringy. It looked like it hadn't been washed in a week. Her eye make-up was smudged, and there were deep circles under her eyes. It was obvious that she hadn't had a decent meal in awhile, and her clothes had spots on them where she had thrown up. If I didn't know better, I would have sworn she lived on the streets.

Mama and I managed to get her cleaned up and get some food in her before meeting with the lawyer. Jeffery, for once, was very helpful and uncharacteristically supportive. He personally called Mr. Taylor and set up the appointment for us. Albert Taylor was very nice but brutally honest. Terry could end up serving some time. Mr. Taylor couldn't be more specific until he had met with the police and the Forrest County District Attorney. Surprisingly, Albert Taylor worked a miracle and got the charges remanded to the file. Two months later, Terry managed to run over a neighbor's mailbox and was discovered with his pants down peeing into the bird feeder. The police found a variety of sleeping pills and pain killers in the back seat of his car. He was sentenced to one year in prison.

My sister was involuntarily committed, which saved her life. Being in treatment and getting away from Terry brought Mary Anne back to us. After six months, she returned home. Mary Anne was ready to get on with her life, but first she wanted to see Terry. I went with her for moral support. What took place made me realize how much Mary Anne had suffered and how much courage it took to make that trip.

The unit that housed Terry resembled a dark cave. I could hear our heels clicking on the hard linoleum floor. The hallway was dimly lit, and I could feel eyes following us to the end of the hall. As we passed the individual cells, I could hear the hard, almost labored, breathing of the men behind those metal doors. Everything was metal: the doors with slits for windows, the stools you sat on, and the tables attached to the gray-colored floors. The visiting area was behind another heavy metal door. There were more metal stools to sit on and telephones to talk on since heavy glass separated the visitors from the inmates.

I almost didn't recognize Terry. He had aged at least ten years and looked about twenty pounds lighter. After a round of hellos, Mary Anne got down to it.

"Terry, you were my great love and I probably would have followed you into hell if you had asked." My sister suddenly laughed and said, "As a matter of fact, I did follow you into hell."

Terry cast his eyes downward and said in almost a whisper, "I'm sorry."

"Oh, I don't blame you," Mary Anne interjected. "I did it to myself; no one else did it to me. I didn't have to take the pills you offered. I didn't have to lose myself in a self destructive haze of pills and booze. You didn't force those pills down my throat."

"No, but…"

"No buts. That's what I'm here for, to tell you that and to forgive you for enabling me. For making it easy for me to do what I have done to myself."

"Thank you, Mary Anne. I know I don't deserve your forgiveness. When I get out of here, it will be different. I promise."

Again, Mary Anne interrupted Terry. "I'm sorry Terry, but it's over. We aren't good for each other. I hope you will change, and I hope you'll have a good life, but it has to be without me."

Terry began to cry and to beg. Even I was unnerved by his obvious pain. But my sister was unyielding. She sat there, repeating the words, "No, Terry," as he tried to change her mind. Finally, it was over. As we walked down the hall and back toward the reception area, Mary Anne began to cry. They were silent tears, streaming down her face, ruining her makeup. There was a haunted look in her eyes. As each metal door slammed shut behind us, my sister jumped. By the time we got to the car, Mary Anne was shaking so hard she seemed to vibrate.

Mary Anne remained in recovery and attended her AA and NA meetings faithfully. She would never be like Lisa, but she certainly was not the Mary Anne I had grown up with. She still loved shopping, jewelry, and all the material things that money could buy. But Mary Anne was now quieter, more reflective, and not so quick to judge. There was sadness in her eyes. Those eyes had seen too much; her life was filled with too many experiences, the bad kind. I felt sorry for her. I was no longer comfortable teasing Mary Anne about her superficial ways and lack of depth. I think my sister would have preferred my criticisms to my new gentleness. It wasn't real, but I couldn't help it.

My marriage continued with the separate beds and the fake love affair that fooled no one. Things rocked along until two events occurred that shook the core of our fragile existence. The first emerged mid-summer. The phone call came in the early afternoon. I could hear the anguish in Betsy's voice.

"I need you. Can you come to Nashville?"

Betsy had followed Doug there after they graduated from college. Everyone thought they would marry. They moved in together instead. My friend put on a brave face, saying she didn't need a legal document to prove they belonged together, but I could tell it bothered her that Doug never proposed.

"Yes, of course. What's going on?" I asked.

"Doug kicked me out," cried Betsy.

"My God, why!"

"I guess because he found an appropriate fiancé, one that his parents would approve of. Plus, I'm pregnant."

"Oh Betsy, I'm so sorry," I exclaimed.

"He said he wanted his children raised as Christians, not half Jews. He said I had to get an abortion; that he wanted nothing to do with it. He called our child an 'it,' Katherine!"

"Betsy, I can't believe…that just doesn't sound like Doug."

"Please come, I need you," my friend pleaded.

"Of course. I'll call back in a few minutes, after I've made plane reservations."

By the time Jeffery arrived home, I was packed and ready to leave for the airport.

"What's this crap about you going to Nashville to be with your Jew friend?"

"Doug kicked Betsy out and she needs me," I said.

"I'm about to make partner and we have social obligations. You can't leave, at least not now," said Jeffery, his voice booming.

Normally I would have given in, but not this time.

"I'm going to be with my friend," I hissed, "and you and your partners can go to hell. You will have to beat me within an inch of my life. That's the only way you can stop me, and if you do, I will either kill you or have you arrested. Now get the hell out of my way, you son-of-a-bitch!"

In a state of shock, Jeffery silently stepped aside. The only sound in that entire house was the slamming of the front door. I practically knocked it off its hinges. After that, I didn't even try to hide my contempt for Jeffery, not even in front of my family.

I took a cab from the airport. The rented condo was dark and still. My friend sat there in the stillness, staring at the wall, saying nothing. I was not prepared for the wreckage I saw in Betsy's face. It wasn't the swollen eyes or the red nose from crying; that was to be expected. It was the look in those swollen eyes that took my breath. It was a look of being flailed alive, of wild, raw, inconsolable pain.

"What happened, Betsy?" I asked.

"Doug broke it off," she said in a whimper.

"But why?" I asked, already knowing most of it from our telephone conversation.

"I'm a Jew and he's a Christian. He said his parents never approved, didn't want me as a daughter-in-law."

"You mean after all these years?" I asked.

"Well, there's the pregnancy and the fact he met someone on one of his business trips. I knew when he came back from Atlanta that things were different."

"How different?" I asked.

"Well, he refused to have sex and made up all kind of ailments to avoid it, and then there were the secret phone calls. He would go in the bathroom and turn on the water. But I could still hear him talking, laughing. He would stay in there for thirty, forty minutes at a time."

"How long did that go on?" I asked, turning on a lamp and leaning forward in order to hear my soft-spoken friend.

"About a month, then all hell broke loose after I listened in on one of his phone conversations. You know I wouldn't do that, not normally, but I knew something was up," explained Betsy.

"Obviously he was talking to the girl he met."

"Yes, her name is Sissy. She's real preppie type. She went to Sewanee, made her debut, all white bread and Anglo-Saxon. And, of course, Doug took her home to meet the parents."

"When did the bastard do that?" I asked, getting madder by the minute.

"Two weekends ago. He insisted that I stay here. He said he had some family business, his Daddy's will and life insurance policies to discuss with both parents."

"I can't believe that sneaky, lousy son-of-a-bitch," I exclaimed.

"Well, that son-of-a-bitch let loose when I confronted him. He said he hadn't loved me for several years but didn't know how to tell me," said Betsy grabbing for another Kleenex. According to my friend, she had already gone through four boxes of Kleenex.

"He said I needed to move out," Betsy continued. "He said he would pay for an abortion, but not one cent if I had it. It -- he called our baby an It," cried Betsy.

"Damn Doug. Damn his parents!" I screamed.

"I should have known! I've never told you this, I was too embarrassed."

"What?" I asked as Betsy seemed to hesitate.

"I was never, and I mean never, invited to Thanksgiving, Christmas, or any family gatherings by Doug's parents."

"You're worth ten of them. I hate them. I could throttle that spineless coward for what he has done!"

Betsy fell into my arms, and I began to cry and rock my friend like a small child who had just awakened from a nightmare. We both rocked and cried until the pain retreated and our tears were spent.

Betsy came home to have the baby. She ended up spending most of her time with me, and Jeffery didn't dare complain. My friend eventually got over Doug and found a nice man who accepted both her and her baby. Betsy never again dated outside her faith. She eventually married Herb and they had three boys.

Next came the death of Frederick Bhaer in late September. Going to his wake and funeral brought up a mountain of conflicted feelings. I seriously considered not going, but I knew I couldn't do that. I rationalized away my fears. David was simply a high school sweetheart, puppy love, and my foreboding was silly at best.

I had not been to the house on North Tisbury since high school. It was a white-washed, wooden home with a small front porch and thin columns supporting an overhang. The living room and dining room were at the front of the house while the family room and kitchen were at the back of the home. The four bedrooms were upstairs.

The den was the heart of the home. It was where the Bhaer family spent most of their time. The den was filled with soft leather chairs, a television, a large brick fireplace and a beige sectional sofa ideal for napping and lounging

As I walked through the front door, I felt the old familiar butterflies. I went through the living room, down the hall, and entered the den where Lee, Phil and David stood in the center of the room. The den was full, overflowing in fact. I had forgotten how many people loved -- not liked, but loved -- Mr. Bhaer. There were pictures of Frederick and his family in every corner of the room. It made my eyes smart to gaze at the captured memories of such a family. Those pictures showed the love they all shared, and now this family was being split apart. Everyone was crying, even my mother. She ran to Lee and hugged her tightly. My father had a dazed, drained look on his face. Frederick's death was so sudden, so unexpected -- a heart attack at work. Mama said he was dead by the time he hit the floor.

After speaking to Lee and Phil, I turned my attention to David. Our eyes locked; I threw my arms around his neck, and he pulled me close. Again, there was the sound of our two hearts beating in unison. I tried to find the right words.

"I'm so sorry. I really don't know what to say other than…"

"Don't say anything. It's okay. In fact, Katie, I would rather you didn't. It's easier that way."

"Okay."

"Listen, let's get out of here for a while. Being alone with you, away from this place, is just what I need right now."

We walked in silence to the public park two blocks away. In the past, the park included a carousel where neighborhood children had spent a nickel to ride wooden horses until their tired mothers would insist it was time to go home. It was also the scene of many Easter egg hunts. Rose Park was aptly named because it was populated with roses of every color: white, red, pink, yellow and burnt orange. In the center of the circular park was a large fountain spraying water at least four feet into the air. On each side of the fountain were wooden benches. As we sat on a bench, near the foundation, we talked and talked, mostly about the past, our past.

"You know, Katie, I've always been lucky, and I've had a charmed life. My parents loved me. I had a father who was a great role model and a supportive older brother. And I guess enough looks, sense and athletic ability to get by."

I interrupted with a laugh and said, "You've got all that in spades…"

"And, I guess, I've been lucky with the girls. I don't understand it, but everything just always fell into place. I've had my share of beautiful women. I've gotten everything in life I've ever wanted, except you, baby."

"You had me, David," I answered.

"And, you were a handful, my love. Different from every girl I've ever met. I noticed that the first time I laid eyes on you. It wasn't just your beauty. You had a wide-eyed innocence which was both compelling and a major turn-off. And then there's your idealism, coupled with a slight dose of uncompromising realism. You saw the ugly without looking away. I found that intriguing. You seemed wiser than most girls your age."

"Not so wise, David, not really," I replied.

David smiled and took my hand in his and said, "At first, Katie, I thought of you as another challenge, another girl to charm. But the longer we dated, the more I cared, the more I wanted you. It became harder and harder to control myself. And you didn't make it any easier. The way you blew hot and cold," he laughed.

"I'm sorry, David. I was so young and so scared," I said.

Looking deep in my eyes, he responded, "I know and I was so young, I didn't understand. Anyway, after Lisa died, you started to withdraw. I just couldn't reach you."

"I know," I said, looking down at my hand enclosed in his.

As David continued, I felt the old familiar pain, that sense of loss that was dormant but still there. "You retreated into a private world of pain. A world I didn't understand. I wanted to comfort you, to ease your grief, but your defenses were so strong. You seemed to shut me out and everything we shared – school, friends, football, dances; everything that made the school year worthwhile. I was quarterback and we were State champs and, Katie, you didn't come to any of the games. I took it pretty hard. After Kennedy died and you retreated into your scrapbooks and memorabilia, I decided I couldn't take it any longer, that I had to break it off."

"I know. I let you down. You don't know how much I regretted that," I confessed.

"Katie, I didn't break it off because I didn't care. I was only seventeen, and I didn't know how to deal with your depression. What you needed was something I couldn't give. I just didn't know how to cope and I was sick of trying."

I felt the tears welling up in my eyes, despite myself. David squeezed my hand and continued, "After we broke up, I dated Patrice to get back at you. And I cheated on her. I probably dated every willing girl in the lower Mississippi Delta. But despite all that, you were still part of me. When I left for Ole Miss in the fall of '64, I believed things would change; that I would finally be able to put you behind me. But then Ray died halfway through our junior year and I knew I would be forced to see you again."

"It wasn't easy for me either." I interjected.

"I know baby, I know. Ray's death brought it all back; the way you closed down after Lisa's death, all that suffering I couldn't cope with. I know I was almost cruel to you at Ray's funeral. I wanted you to believe I no longer cared."

"I did believe you."

"It was a lie, Katie. I still cared. I still loved you. I went back to college and got on with it. But I still thought of you. The years passed and I heard you got married. I tried to convince myself that things were too difficult with us, too many challenges. I told myself that we were so young and everything was so overwhelming, or seemed so."

"So you joined the Air Force after graduating?"

"Yes," David answered. "That was about the time my frat brother, Evan, died of cancer."

"I heard you took him to Florida."

"Yes, we took one last road trip together. We drove to Ft. Lauderdale, despite the fact that Evan was already suffering from the effects of his disease. He could barely walk or dress himself, so I played nurse."

"That was sweet of you," I said, looking deep into David's eyes, wanting to put my arms around him.

"I'm glad I went -- that Evan had time near the ocean he loved so much. We arrived after dark, so I helped Evan undress and get into bed. Then I fixed myself a drink, sat on the back porch of the beach house we had rented for the week, and thought about my friend that was sleeping inside."

"It must have been hard for you, seeing your friend like that."

"It was. Evan and I went through Rush together. We were in the same pledge class and were like brothers throughout college. We took road trips together. Those were carefree days with no thoughts of the future except that it lay unending before us. Little did I know…"

"It's funny how quickly things can change," I said.

"Yes, it is. Evan discovered his cancer as a result of a visit to his local dentist, who then sent him to a specialist where the cancer was diagnosed. Amazingly enough, Evan, who didn't have a serious thought in his head, began to prepare himself for the end. He talked about his death dispassionately. He told me how he wanted to deal with each stage of his disease and what he expected from his friends. He was very courageous."

"He sounds like it."

"He didn't shy away from any aspect of his impending demise. I, on the other hand, had a hard time dealing with the fact Evan was dying. It brought me face to face with my own mortality."

"I understand that feeling."

"Yes, I know you do. You know, Katie, many of Evan's old friends avoided him."

"You're kidding. That's awful, David."

"I agree. Those cowards were uncomfortable around him."

"Tell me more about the trip," I asked.

"Well, the morning after we arrived was a good one. We hit the beach early, and Evan's face lit up when he saw the blue water and white sand. We sat on towels and talked about what we would do for the next six days and where and what we would eat. Evan thanked me for everything, and I told him not to mention it. If the shoe had been on the other foot, he would have done the same thing for me. I was glad I was able to give him one last visit to the beach. At the end of the day, I lifted him up and carried him to the water.

"Were you with him at the end?" I asked.

"Yes. Evan went blind and then slipped into a coma. It was then that I began to understand what you went through with Lisa's death. I wanted to pick up the phone and call you, but I knew I didn't have the right. Then I got the news about Dad. One phone call and I was never the same. My Dad was my hero, my friend, and the one person I could count on, no matter what. Katie, I felt lost and afraid. The pain was so strong it hurt physically. Evan's death and now Dad's death was like an unwelcome guest who refused to leave. I was in a detached fog until I saw you again."

With that, David put his arm around my shoulder and pulled me close to him. I looked into his eyes and saw sadness, longing, and love. I'm sure he saw the same thing in my face. That night we made love for the first time. David followed me back to Jackson. Jeffery was out of town, trying a case in north Mississippi. I guess I should have felt guilty, having sex with someone other than my husband. But I didn't. I knew I didn't love Jeffery and that it had been years since we acted like man and wife. What I did feel was love, overwhelming, intense, and unconditional love for David.

He told me the minute we touched that he felt alive again. He said making love to me was different from anything he had ever felt before. The mental pleasure David said he felt was as great as the physical enjoyment, an enjoyment greater and more intense than anything he had ever experienced. I felt the same way. We were both so hungry -- hungry for one another. It was a hunger that built over so many years and lasted so long. It nearly consumed us.

After the funeral, David went back to San Diego and from there to Germany. He had been in the Air Force since college. He had one more year to serve. We wrote and made plans. I would divorce Jeffery, and we would finally start a life together. David wrote me every day and called me long distance every night. We couldn't wait to be together again.

And then Mama told me her secret. Actually, I found the letters and she confirmed my worst fears. It happened two months after David left for Germany.

I was home for the weekend. It's funny how a particular act can affect a whole series of events. If only I hadn't been looking for a piece of paper to jot down a telephone number.

If only I hadn't answered the telephone. If only I hadn't found those letters from Frederick. There were five letters, all hidden underneath Mama's address book in the middle of her bedside table. The endearments on the front of each envelope drove me to read the contents and learn things I never knew and things I wish I didn't know.

I don't know how long I had been sitting on Mama's bed when she walked in. The letters were still in my lap and it was obvious I had read them.

"Why?" I asked.

"Katherine, I didn't mean for it to happen. If you read all the letters, then you know my past," said Mama, her voice cracking.

She talked about her childhood, her life with my grandmother, Grace, and how safe she finally felt when Grace married Mama's step-father, Ralph.

Mama continued, her hands shaking. By now, we were both shaking with emotion.

"So why did you leave West Virginia?" I asked. "Didn't you tell Daddy you left the mountains at sixteen?"

"Yes, I did, and that's true. The reason is Ralph's younger brother, Joe. He came to live with us."

"And there wasn't enough room? Is that why you left?"

I could tell by the way Mama hesitated that what she was about to tell me wasn't good. I almost wished I hadn't pressed her.

"No, honey, that's not it" With tears welling in Mama's eyes and with a deep sigh, she told me her darkest and most painful secret.

"I was attacked in the woods. Joe raped me. I was only fourteen. Oh, God, I can't do this," she said, covering her eyes with her hands, trying not to cry out loud.

I watched Mama while she wept and remembered. I wanted to reach out to her but I was afraid to. After Mama calmed down, she continued, "It was brutal and bloody. I tried to fight but he kicked me in the stomach until I couldn't stand the pain. I told your grandmother and her response was to drink!"

"Oh my God," I cried, horrified and numb with shock at

what I was hearing.

"The second time, he almost broke my ribs. It happened repeatedly for the next two years. I finally couldn't take it any longer and left home at sixteen."

Wiping the tears from my eyes and trying not to lose it completely, I asked, "Did you ever hear from Ralph or your mother after you left?"

"Years later, I received a poorly written letter from Ralph. Mother's liver finally gave out."

"Mama, how horrible. I had no idea!"

"How could you? I never wanted you to know, but then you found the letters."

"What happened after you left the mountains?"

"I managed to find work and support myself," she explained. "But I never finished high school. I vowed that if I ever had children, they would get an education. I was determined that y'all weren't going to suffer the way I had."

"So when did you meet the boy who brought you to Mississippi?" I asked, wondering about those intervening years Mama rarely talked about.

"At eighteen, I met Michael. He was the love of my life. I couldn't believe that a man as good as Michael wanted me. We planned to marry after he graduated from University of Kentucky, but Pearl Harbor changed everything. Michael enlisted and was sent to Camp Shelby near Hattiesburg for training."

"So you followed him to Mississippi?"

"Yes," she said. "I wanted to spend as much time as I could with Michael before he was shipped overseas."

"I would do the same, Mama. I would follow David to another state, even another county."

"You never stopped loving him, did you?"

"No, Mama."

"Well, I loved Michael as much as you love David. I moved during the middle of April. May and June were hot and miserable, but I didn't care. I was young and all that mattered was being with him. Those three months I spent with Michael were incredible. After he died, I moved to Lancaster and went to work as a bank teller. It was your father's bank. It wasn't long before we were dating. Tom took me to fancy restaurants and bombarded me with expensive gifts."

"Pretty heady stuff for a girl from West Virginia," I interjected.

"Your father and I were not well matched. We didn't love each other, at least not then. I was still grieving over the boy I lost during the war and your father wanted to get even with his parents. They stopped him from marrying his high school sweetheart when he was only seventeen."

"So how did all this lead to your affair with Fredrick?"

"He was there when Tom subjected me to the final humiliation. After that we dropped all pretense of caring for each other. I'm sorry, Katie, I know this is hard…"

"That's the first time you called me Katie."

Ignoring my observation, Mama continued.

"Because of Tom's drinking we didn't go out much or socialize. But Lee's party was the exception. Tom got drunk and I caught him having sex with Lee's younger sister, his high school sweetheart. It seems they started seeing each other shortly after I married your father."

"How do you know that?" I asked.

"After I caught him in the act, he confessed everything. He told me he had never loved me. He said the only reason he stayed with me was because of you girls."

"I'm sorry, Mama."

"It's not the fact he didn't love me. It's the way he told me, the cruelty of it. Frederick knew everything. Thank God Lee didn't. He knew I was hurting. At first it was one friend comforting another and then it gradually grew into something more. We both felt so guilty and broke it off. And then I discovered I was pregnant with twins."

"You must have been frantic!"

"I was. I tricked your father into having sex with me. I know that wasn't very nice, but it was better than splitting up two families, and your father was beside himself with the thought of more children, possibly sons."

"Did anyone know?"

"Yes, Lisa and, of course, Frederick. They kept my secret."

"Mama, did you love Frederick?"

"In a way yes. Not like the boy I lost during the war. But yes, in a way. I never wanted you to know for so many reasons, not the least of which was David."

"It's ironic that you would mention David," I said, tears filling my eyes, overflowing.

Mama reached out and touched my hand. This was an act of kindness that seemed foreign to her nature, at least to me. With her hand in mine, I continued.

"I can't judge, since I did the same thing. Like you, I married a man I didn't love and I'm having an affair with David. The difference is I plan to leave Jeffery and marry David, or at least I did.'

"And now you're not so sure?"

"I don't know how David's going to take the fact that my brothers are his brothers and the fact that his father and my mother had an affair."

"Why tell him when you know it could spoil so many lives? Katie, think about it."

"No one will know except David. Mama, I can't lie to him. I just can't."

"What about you? What if David can't handle the truth?"

"I just can't keep this from him," I explained. "I wouldn't know how. David knows me too well. He would know somehow. He would eventually figure it out."

"I only hope you know what you're doing. In any case, I'm here if you need me. And Katie, I'm so sorry."

With that, we did something unusual - we embraced.

I went through the full gamut of emotions after my discovery of the letters. I felt empathy, as well as red hot anger, towards Mama. I also felt connected to her for the first time in my short life. There was anger and disappointment at my father, who had been my hero, the perfect male, whom all other males were measured against. But the overriding emotion was fear – fear for what it would do to my relationship with David. Lastly, there was the fear of what this terrible knowledge would do to David personally.

I couldn't get past the pain it would cause him. His father was David's hero. He had idolized the man all his life. And now I held the power to destroy David's memory of him. Nothing else mattered but David. True, I was disappointed in Mama and Daddy. But all those secrets she kept for so many years actually brought us closer together. And Daddy had since made up for some of his mistakes. He and Mama had grown to depend on one another, and "wonder of wonders," felt true affection for each other. But none of that could remove the conflict or anxiety I felt. Whatever I did, it would hurt David. My problem was deciding what would hurt him less.

I thought back to the many conversations David and I had about Frederick. I remembered one in particular. We were parked by the levee enjoying a summer breeze when he said, "Katie, my Dad taught me to throw a football, play tennis and golf. I learned to drive because of him. I owe him a lot."

Those words were now haunting me. I decided not to say or do anything until David came home from Germany. The months passed slowly. The nights were a relentless procession of

146

floor pacing and tossing in my bed. Finally, the waiting was over and all decisions had been made. I did what I thought was best for David. My love for him dictated my actions. There was no turning back.

We met at my parent's house. My heart began to pound when I heard his car turn into the driveway. As David crossed the threshold into the den, I rushed into his arms. We kissed for several minutes, each kiss longer and more intense that the last. I could hear his heart beating in unison with mine. David was the first to pull away, laughing and saying we had plenty of time for that sort of thing.

I shook my head and said, "No, my love, we don't, and make no mistake, you are my love – my only love."

David looked puzzled and disturbed when he asked, "Katie, what the hell are you talking about?"

"I can't see you again," I sobbed.

His face went white and his eyes darkened.

"Again? What the hell are you talking about?" he asked, his hands now firmly on my shoulders.

"Jeffery and I have decided to give it another try – to make our marriage work."

"Katie, I don't understand. You told me you never should have married Jeffery and that you never loved him. What gives, Katie?"

"Jeffery and I have decided to give it one more try," I repeated. "David, I took vows. Marriage is serious…"

"I know that, but you don't love him. You never did or were you lying to me?" asked David, his voice suddenly harsh.

"David, I have to try. I told him I would," I interjected.

"What about us, Katie? You know how I feel, and I thought I knew how you felt."

"I can't," I cried, unable to continue.

In a flash he was gone. I sat down on the sofa and stared into space, too numb to move. Suddenly, Mama was in the room holding me.

"Katie, I'm sorry."

"Mama, it's killing me but I had to let him go; to protect him," I said, shaking my head in disbelief over what had just happened.

"Are you sure? Is this really what you want?"

"No, but I have no choice," I responded.

"What now?" Mama asked.

"I don't know," I answered. "I can't make any more decisions. I'm too upset!"

I sat there in the den with Mama until it grew dark. I called Jeffery and told him I was spending the night at my parent's house. Mama and Daddy did their best to comfort me, but nothing could ease the agony I was feeling. I went through the motions of living. I did what I needed to do but with tired eyes and a broken heart. I was like a lifeless robot, without joy or animation. Even clueless Jeffery noticed and asked what was wrong with me.

"Nothing. Not a damned thing. Life is great, just great. What could possibly be wrong? I have such a wonderful, loving husband -- a husband that anticipates my every need and moves heaven and earth to make me happy!" I screamed, the venom and hate evident in my voice. My rage was so intense that Jeffery gave me a wide berth and left me alone when I wanted privacy. That was the only good thing to come out of all that pain.

What finally brought me out of my grief was the twins. My brothers brought me back to myself. It was hard to be sad or angry when those two were around. I wondered if I was wrong to deny David the companionship of his half-brothers.

I couldn't help but think of David when Quentin was on the pitcher's mound, throwing his lethal curve ball or when Daniel defeated the state champion in a hard fought doubles match. As they grew older, the twins reminded more and more of David. They both had his lanky frame, broad shoulders and graceful gait. It saddened me to think that David would never have the opportunity to play catch with them or share experiences on the gridiron or tell them what it was like to fly a plane.

One day, when I was particularly bombarded with memories of him, I asked Mama if I had made a terrible mistake. We were watching Quentin represent Lancaster High in a state-wide swim meet when I asked for her input.

"Mama, did I do the right thing when I broke it off with David? I mean, I denied him the chance to know his half-brothers."

"Katherine, I can't tell you whether your decision was right or wrong. Only you know that. It was your decision. Baby, why are you second-guessing yourself now?"

"I don't know. When I look at Daniel and Quentin, I can't help but think of David and how much he's missing," I explained.

"If there's one thing I've learned is that you can't go back and do it over. You did what you thought was right at the time. Your motives were pure. That's the best you can hope for, Katherine. You have to go on with your life and let go of the past," Mama advised.

She was right, and that's just what I tried to do.

When my daughter found the letters, I cried for days until my eyes were almost swollen shut. Then I prayed and prayed some more. I asked God not to take my sins out on my daughter. Thank goodness Tom was away at a banking convention. Otherwise, how would I explain the red eyes and the erratic behavior? After re-reading my letters from Fred several times, I burned those sweet notes. It was difficult but I didn't want anyone else to discover what my lover had written, especially Tom.

After several days of soul-searching, I called Katherine and asked her to come over for lunch. I didn't want my daughter to make any decisions until she had time to think things out and listen to my input. I hoped I could somehow correct some of the damage those letters had caused. We sat on the patio under the shade of a large oak. As I picked at my chicken salad, I asked Katherine if she had made any decision about David. She informed me that she would either tell him about Frederick and me or break it off with him.

"Katherine, you can't do that!" I exclaimed.

"Why not?"

"Because you love each other, and I don't want y'all to break up because of what happened between Fred and me."

"Mama, you should have thought of that before you plunged head-long into an affair with your best friend's husband!" she responded with an edge in her voice.

"I know I deserve that, and if I could undo what I did, I would. But honey, I can't. Please don't let this destroy everything," I begged.

With that, my daughter explained there was no way she could keep such a secret from David. For days, Katherine alternated between breaking it off and telling David the truth. Finally, she told me she would tell David about his father's affair with me after he returned from Germany. Her decision didn't seem to give her any peace of mind. I felt such guilt and tried to comfort her. Sometimes, Katherine would accept my attempts to soothe her. Other times, she would lash out in frustration and anger. I didn't blame her.

Tom could tell something was wrong and asked me on several occasions what was bothering me. Each time I blew him off by saying I didn't feel well; always a headache or stomach ache I couldn't get rid of. One day, he said something that put an end to my charade. We were sitting in the backyard; Tom was reading the paper and I was drinking a cola. It was late afternoon and I was commenting on the beauty of the autumn leaves when he interrupted me.

"What's going on between you and Katie?" he asked.

"I don't know what you mean."

"Yes, you do. I see the tension between you two and I've noticed the whispering. Every time I walk into a room, I notice it and suddenly the whispering stops. So what's up?"

"She wants to divorce Jeffery and marry David when he gets out of the Air Force."

"Yes, I know. She told me. Pat, I'm not stupid. It's more than that and you know it."

"She's having second thoughts about whether she should leave Jeffery," I said, refusing to look Tom in the eyes. But he wasn't fooled by my answer.

"Pat, does it have anything to do with your affair with Fred?"

I dropped the container I was holding and began to shake after the glass shattered on the patio brick.

"It's okay, Pat," my husband continued. "I've known for years and have long-since forgiven you," he said, reaching for my hand and squeezing it.

"How…how did you find out?" I stuttered.

"Fred told me."

"What exactly did he say?" I asked, fearing he now knew the secret about the twins.

"Just that you had a short affair after you discovered I was cheating on you with my high school sweetheart. So I don't blame you. I know you were hurting and very angry."

"And you forgave me, just like that?"

"No," he laughed. "It took awhile. Anyway, does Katie know about you and Fred?"

"Yes."

As we continued to talk, I realized that Fred had told Tom half the truth. I didn't have the heart to tell him the rest. Later, I asked my daughter not to reveal the rest of it.

She agreed, saying "What would be the point in hurting Daddy? There's enough hurt as it is. Besides, he's so proud of the twins and he's their father. Daddy's the one who raised them all these years," she reasoned.

"Thank you, honey. I'm not asking for myself but for your father."

"Yes, and that's why I'm agreeing," she responded. "Daddy's changed, and he deserves a break -- something the rest of us are not getting."

All I could say was "I'm sorry." I said it over and over again, thinking at least this is the end of it. What else could happen? I asked myself.

I was soon to find out. When David came home from Germany, Katherine dropped her bombshell. When he stormed out of the house and turned the corner on two wheels, I knew what Katherine had done. She gave up the man she loved in order to protect him. All I could do was comfort her and ask Katherine, Tom and God to forgive me. Every time I looked into my daughter's tortured eyes, I felt immense guilt. Gradually, Katherine began to come out of her cloud of misery. She immersed herself in family activities, especially when those activities involved the twins. Their laughter and youthful antics made her happy. Even Jeffery did what he could to appease her, despite the fact Katherine made no attempt to hide her contempt for him. Her feelings for Jeffery were pretty obvious at the annual picnic Tom and I held each year for family and friends.

I had asked Katherine to bring the hamburger patties outside for grilling. As she entered the den, I called out, "Don't forget the potato salad, as well."

She yelled back, "I'll ask my idiot husband to bring it. I've got my hands full."

What surprised me was that he didn't take the bait, but meekly followed behind his wife, bringing the potato salad with him. As soon as it was feasible to do so, I pulled Katherine aside and said, "What in the world is going on? I can't believe you insulted Jeffery in front of God and everybody!"

"That's not all I intend to say if he even looks at me funny. I'm sick of him and I don't intend to pretend otherwise."

"Katherine, people will talk. You can't act that way in public."

"Mama, do you really think I care if people know my marriage is a farce?" she asked.

Despite our talk, my daughter refused to rein in her animosity toward Jeffery, and people did begin to talk. At my wits end, Tom and I asked Katherine to meet us at a small Italian restaurant near her Belhaven home.

As Katherine took her seat, I started in. "Honey, I know you're going through a difficult time…"

"We both do," interrupted Daddy.

"But you're going to have to control your emotions. It's one thing to show your contempt for Jeffery around family, but it's quite another thing when you do it in public."

"Yesterday, one of my long-standing customers asked me if you and Jeffery were getting a divorce," said Daddy, shaking his head.

"If you're that miserable, maybe you should at least separate, since you're not ready to involve yourself in a 'messy divorce', as you put it," I suggested.

"I'm sorry. You're right, but a separation is not necessary right now. I've been taking my grief over David out on Jeffery, and it's not been fair to anyone."

After that, things settled down, and I almost forgot the suffering I had caused, but not quite. I was still amazed at Tom's willingness to forgive me. One night at Angie's, I brought it up. Tom and I were enjoying our Sunday night helping of fried shrimp and lemon icebox pie when I said, "I still can't believe you've forgiven me for my affair with Frederick."

"It took awhile but after a time, I began to realize that I drove you into the arms of Fred. I wasn't much of a husband."

"You've more than made up for that, Tom," I said, smiling at him.

"I also realized that I loved you and never wanted to risk losing you again."

As we walked toward the car, I stopped my husband and put my arms around him and asked, "Who are you, and what have you done with Tom?"

Chapter Twenty Five
JANUARY 18, 1983

When David and I broke up, Quentin and Daniel were sixteen. The years passed and they grew into young men. I stayed with Jeffery in our loveless marriage. My only joy in those intervening years was watching my baby brothers grow up. I never missed a birthday, a tennis match, a baseball game or their graduations, high school and college.

Quentin was a natural athlete but Daniel had to work at it. By the time Quentin was eight years old, he was proficient at golf and tennis, as well as being a superb swimmer. Daniel was a runner. In high school, he was on the track team and one of the best running backs to graduate from Lancaster High. Both were outgoing and seemed as comfortable with adults as with children their own age, just like David. Even when they were very young, there was something about their mannerisms and the way they walked that reminded me of my former love. They both had the same long legs and broad shoulders but their coloring was different from him. It is funny how my brothers reminded me so much of David. Of course, that was before I knew the truth. I chalked it up to missing him; he was always in my thoughts.

Quentin loved to read. He would go to the local library and bring home five books a week and read every one of them. Daniel loved to paint. He had a natural talent and spent hours drawing various members of the family. When no one was available, he would draw Gordon, the lab, or Annie, the cat.

The boys spent a lot of weekends with me in Jackson. Jeffery didn't seem to mind, maybe because their company put me in a good mood. When the boys visited, the tension between Jeffery and me seemed to lessen. They would run up the front steps two at a time and yell, "Hey, Sis – where are 'ya?" They turned on the television--sporting events, of course--and the stereo and talked over each other in an attempt to tell me what they had done at school the week before. They filled my house with lots of noise and laughter, and I loved every minute of it. I especially enjoyed cooking for them. I never cooked for Jeffery. He went out every night and didn't return until late. I used the boys as guinea pigs and tried out new recipes. They ate whatever I put in front of them and always asked for seconds. In a way, my brothers were like the children I never had.

As the twins got older, they developed very distinct and individual personalities. Quentin emerged as the star of the family. My father loved to brag about his athletic exploits and Mama was convinced that Quentin would be governor one day. None of this bothered Daniel; sibling rivalry was nonexistent between the boys. Daniel was proud of his brother, and Quentin encouraged and supported Daniel's artistic pursuits. It made me smile to watch them together. They had a way of looking out for each other that reminded me of the relationship I had with Lisa. It was Daniel watching his brother's back that saved Quentin from tragic consequences.

It all began their sophomore year at Lancaster High. The first day of school, Quentin befriended a guy named Lester Sharp. He wasn't anything like Quentin. Daniel said Lester looked like a short version of Colonel Reb and had the personality of a pet rock. According to Daniel, Lester acted as if he were observing people under a microscope, and it was obvious he didn't like what he saw.

"Sis, you wouldn't believe it. He sniffs his food before he eats it. I guess Lester thinks someone's going to poison him, but who would bother? He's not worth it," laughed Daniel.

"Your brother seems to like him," I said.

"That's what bothers me," said Daniel. "I don't trust that guy."

Lester followed Quentin around like a little puppy dog. Quentin's other friends, along with Daniel, were irritated by Lester's actions. According to Daniel, Lester invited himself to every gathering and then sat in silence watching Quentin like a hawk. He thought nothing of starting a fight. Whenever somebody cracked a joke, voiced an opinion, or made an observation, Quentin's new friend would make some smug comment. Lester was the master of the put-down, letting people know that he thought little of that individual's intelligence or character.

One incident stood out in Daniel's memory. Sam, a friend of the twins since grade school, mentioned how he was looking forward to spring try-outs and hoping he would make the football team. Lester jumped in with both feet and implied that Sam had better wear a helmet during practice since he couldn't afford any more damage to his brain. Sam, red-faced, took a swing at Lester. Daniel told me Quentin grabbed Sam's hand just in time. Otherwise, Lester would have been toast. Quentin was always coming to Lester's defense, figuratively and literally; this was something Daniel couldn't understand.

Even Lester's girlfriend was a reflection of his disagreeable personality. She was a mousey little thing with short stumps for legs, a flat-chest, and usually sullen. The only time Janice showed any emotion was when Lester focused his sarcasm on her. She got bug-eyed, her bottom lip trembled, and she developed a noticeable twitch in her right eye. Daniel told me he felt sorry for her and wondered why Janice subjected herself to Lester's verbal abuse.

Daniel felt Quentin's new friend was using him because of Quentin's popularity, a fact Daniel found ironic considering Lester's antisocial behavior. He told me he didn't feel that Lester was capable of being a real friend to anyone.

The truth came out the night of the Spring Fling. Lester insisted that Quentin and his date ride with him to the dance. Daniel, not as naïve as his brother, was nervous about the arrangement Quentin had with Lester. He told me that the last few times he had been around Lester, the guy's eyes were unfocused and he was very loud and extremely talkative. At first, Daniel thought Lester was drunk, but he didn't smell any alcohol on him. Concerned for his brother, Daniel talked Quentin into giving him and his date a ride to the Spring Fling. When Quentin arrived at Lester's house with Daniel and his date in the backseat, Lester threw a fit.

"What the hell is he doing here? There's no room," he bellowed. "Quentin, are you and Daniel connected at the hip? Look, man, I know you're twins, but this is ridiculous."

"I think I'd better go," said Quentin, quickly backing away from Lester.

As Quentin got into the car, Daniel said, "That's what I was afraid of, bro. There's something wrong with that guy. You need to cut him loose."

Quentin agreed, and as he pulled out of the driveway, he saw Lester standing next to his car. His hands were curled into tight fists, his eyes black holes, and his mouth spewing obscenities. His date was wild-eyed; her body shook uncontrollably. My brothers and their dates rode to the dance in shocked silence.

As they were leaving the dance, they heard sirens all the way from the Armory. Quentin followed the sounds, which led him to a ditch just outside of town. Inside the ditch was the crushed metal of Lester's car. The bodies of Lester and his date, Janice, were still inside. Later, the autopsies on their bodies revealed that Lester had a combination of drugs in his system, including PCP and heroin, and Janice had been severely beaten prior to the accident. Her injuries included a broken nose and a shattered jaw.

Daniel's sophomore year was also the year that my brother fell in love for the first and last time. The day after Daniel met Beth, he told me about their meeting. Everything he felt for Beth was exactly what I had felt for David. I knew my baby brother had met the girl he would spend the rest of his life with, or at least I hoped he would, and not make the same mistakes I had made.

"Sis, she's pretty, really pretty, and she's so sweet. You're gonna love her. I met her in Art Class."

Beth sat next to Daniel and asked him if he had an extra charcoal pencil. Her clear blue eyes took in every inch of him, which made Daniel blush. My brother handed her the pencil and managed to learn her entire history in the span of ten minutes. Beth, like Daniel, came from a large family. She was the youngest of seven, five girls and two boys. Her father, Jim, was a chemical engineer who worked for a local plant that made fertilizer for farmers in Mississippi and the surrounding states. Her mother was a legal secretary who had worked since Beth was in preschool. The fact that Jean had a job was an oddity since most mothers were stay-at-home moms. Beth said her family needed the extra money, so her mother took the only job available: secretary to a local attorney. Despite this fact, her family members were very close and did everything together. Every holiday, and especially every birthday, was a major event; attendance by all was mandatory. Each year, Beth's father would plan a vacation that was both fun and educational. One year they all went to Yellowstone Park, the next year Boston, and the year after that SeaWorld in Orlando, Florida. Beth was one of the funniest, most well-adjusted individuals I had ever met. Her family and her upbringing obviously had a positive influence on Beth. I envied her and wished my family had been as normal and happy, with no secrets to hide and no shame to repress. By the end of class, Daniel had asked Beth to the Saturday midnight show and she had accepted. She became Daniel's "rock," his confidant, and his most avid supporter. We all loved her, Quentin included.

During their junior year, Quentin was elected Class President, Class Favorite, and Captain of the football team. He also caught the eye of a pretty brunette named Laurie. The twins and their girls did everything together. I had joked that it was a good thing that Beth and Laurie got along, considering they were forced to spend most of their waking hours together!

Likewise, I enjoyed spending time with the girls. Who else would watch Diana and Prince Charles' wedding with me or care "Who Shot J.R.?" Certainly not the twins or Jeffrey. Beth and Laurie, to their credit, withstood the unmerciful teasing of my brothers. I reminded the boys that not everyone liked Saturday night wrestling, not to mention every John Wayne movie ever made.

When the twins spent the weekends with me, their girlfriends were invited for Saturday cookouts. This routine continued throughout high school and college. After dinner, we would play Trivial Pursuit and end the evening falling asleep in front of the television while watching John Wayne save the day. I'm sure the boys could have spent their nights elsewhere, but I was grateful they spent those nights with me. It filled an otherwise silent house with lots of wonderful sounds.

In his senior year at Lancaster High, Quentin led the football team to a State Championship. The entire family watched and cheered as Quentin ran forty yards for a touchdown, securing the lead in the last three minutes of the fourth quarter and winning the game. That was the year that Daniel entered an art contest and won. He received an art scholarship to Belhaven and had his first exhibition at a local gallery in Jackson.

Since disco dancing was popular, Jeffery and I gave the twins a Disco Party as a graduation present. Everybody danced to songs from Saturday Night Fever and all the boys dressed like John Travolta.

The summer after graduation, Quentin campaigned for Jason Clark, the first black to run for mayor of Lancaster. Of course, Jeffery was furious, but I told him to mind his own damn business. I thought when Daniel joined Quentin in making phone calls and handing out campaign buttons that Mama would object, but she didn't! Only Jeffery spoke out – terrified that members of his firm would disapprove.

Several days after my latest skirmish with my husband over the campaign, I visited Jason Clark's campaign office. I spotted Quentin right away. He was handing out campaign buttons and brochures to other volunteers for distribution in front of the Piggly-Wiggly and other local businesses. Daniel was busy manning the phones. Surprising even myself, I asked if there was anything I could do.

"Hi, Sis," said Quentin, waving me over. "You sure can; how about making a few phone calls?"

"Okay, do you have a list?"

"Yes, I sure do," laughed Quentin. "I'll let you start with the B's and you can go from there."

I spent the rest of the day at the campaign office. I went back the following day and the day after that, but it was nothing compared to the work my brothers did. They worked tirelessly right up to the election. The other thing that surprised me was that there were other white volunteers. They were mostly college age and their numbers were small, but it still gave me hope that things were changing.

Jason Clark had a good showing but didn't win. Of course, Jeffery was relieved. I reminded him that change was coming and that he had better get used to it. His answer was an angry glare and a slam of the door.

Not long after election night, I had lunch with Mama. She was finishing her turtle soup and I was munching on my spinach salad when I asked, "Mama, I'm surprised you didn't raise unmitigated hell when Quentin and Daniel joined Jason Clark's campaign."

"How could I when three out of my four surviving children campaigned for him?" she responded. "Besides, I gave up on trying to control my children a long time ago. You all are much too hard-headed to be controlled," she laughed.

"Well, bless my soul, Mama! I do believe you've changed your spots after all these years."

"Katherine, are you calling me a leopard?"

"Yes, but a much improved one," I said with a smirk.

"Don't get cute."

Ignoring her retort, I continued my observation. "There was a time when you would have screamed, cried, and even resorted to physical violence for a lot less provocation."

"Katherine, those were different times. What you don't understand was that your outspoken views could have gotten all of us in trouble."

"That still doesn't explain your change of heart. Back then, all you needed was a white sheet!"

"You still don't pull any punches, do you?" responded Mama, obviously smarting from my comments.

"I guess I don't. It's just that you've changed so much. I was wondering why."

"Katie, I still don't believe the way you do, but I know if Quentin and Daniel had been around during that voter registration thing, they would have been in the thick of it."

"You're probably right," I commented.

"I can't help but think about the mothers of those three civil rights workers," Mama continued. "I can only imagine how I would have felt if my boys had been shot and buried in a dam."

Later, I thought about my conversation with Mama. I realized that people do change a little at a time. Sometimes the change is so subtle that you don't notice at first and sometimes that change has to be forced.

After high school graduation, the twins enrolled at Belhaven College in Jackson. Both were on the tennis team and played baseball their sophomore and junior years. By their senior year, Daniel knew he wanted to be a commercial artist and Quentin had decided to go to law school. We, that is, his family, knew it was a stepping stone to a political career - the Governor's Mansion and maybe the U.S. Senate.

Early in the boys' senior year, there were engagement and wedding plans for the summer of 1983. Daniel presented Beth with a diamond solitaire and she fell into his arms after saying yes. All of us were beside ourselves. Only Quentin didn't seem excited. He excused himself from the family celebration of the news and said he was going to bed. Quentin had been sick for several days with what appeared to be a bad stomach virus. I told him if it wasn't better in a couple of days, he needed to see Dr. Pierce and get something to stop the nausea. He agreed.

"Okay, sis, I think I need something to stop the pain in the pit of my stomach."

Growing more concerned, I demanded he see the doctor the next morning.

"Okay, sis, okay! I'll go see Dr. Pierce, I promise."

With that, I kissed him good-night and rejoined the celebration.

Chapter Twenty Six
JANUARY 20, 1983

I was sitting in front of the television set watching Ronald Reagan, a former actor, take the oath of office. Despite the deaths of the Kennedys, Martin Luther King, Watergate, and the Iran hostage crisis, I still couldn't believe that Ronald Reagan was President. Some things just didn't seem possible. But there I was with my big hair and padded shoulders watching Reagan become President of the United States. As I marveled over the strange turn of events I was witnessing, the telephone rang. It was my father. His voice had that same painful, hollow sound I had heard once before, the night Lisa died.

My father didn't mince words. "Baby, I'm sorry, Quentin is dead, complications from a ruptured appendix. When it burst, sepsis set in," said Daddy, trying not to cry into the phone. Around three o'clock this morning I heard him scream. We rushed him to the hospital but it was too late. He was too far gone," cried Daddy, practically choking on his own words.

I let out a piercing scream and dropped the phone. I don't remember much after that, since I was heavily sedated and in shock. The fog didn't lift until several days after the funeral.

A month later, Beth called and asked if we could meet for lunch. I suggested a little Italian restaurant located two blocks from the Medical Center. Tony's was softly lit with red checkered tablecloths and fresh daisies in Mason jars strategically placed in the center of each table. The green walls were decorated with scenes from Venice, Rome, and the Amalfi coast. I arrived early and ordered two glasses of Merlot. I figured we would need it!

As Beth walked toward our table, nestled in a corner close to the entrance, I could tell she was upset, and I knew the reason why.

"How's Daniel?" I asked.

"Not good; that's why I called," explained Beth.

"I guessed that."

"He sits for hours in the dark. He breaks dates with me, and when I try to talk to him about Quentin, he shuts me out. Beth reached for a Kleenex in her purse and continued. "He's cut every class for the last two weeks. If Daniel doesn't stop cutting classes, he could flunk out!"

"But his grades have been so good; he's on the President's List," I exclaimed, becoming more and more concerned. As Beth picked at her food, she told me that my brother was beyond grieving and that she couldn't help him.

Reaching for the wine, I said, "Do you want me to talk to him?"

"Would you?" Beth asked, obviously relieved. "He listens to you."

As we left the restaurant, I promised to call my little brother that same afternoon.

When Daniel didn't answer his phone, I went to his apartment and found him sitting in the dark with the television on, oblivious to the noise. I invited myself in and got right to the point.

"Baby, I know you're hurting but you can't give up. Quentin wouldn't want that."

"Sis, you don't understand," said my brother, his eyes staring into space.

"You're wrong, Daniel. I know exactly what you're feeling and I understand all too well. Shall I explain?" I asked.

"Whatever," said Daniel, not convinced.

"I know you were too young to remember Lisa but she was more than a sister to me. She was my friend, my confidante, my protector. If I was feeling bad, I could go to my sister and tell her whatever was bothering me and instantly feel better." My eyes began to water as I continued to tell Daniel about the sister he never knew. "If Lisa hadn't been my sister, we still would have been friends; best friends, in fact. There was no one I enjoyed spending time with more than her."

"That's how I felt about Quentin," said Daniel.

I nodded and continued my story. "When Lisa died, I felt like someone had reached inside me, pulled out my heart, and smashed it. I didn't care about anything. My junior year was a complete wash-out. I didn't go to any of the dances or football games even though my boyfriend was the quarterback. I lost the love of my life because of my endless grieving."

"You mean the love of your life wasn't Jeffery?" said Daniel, laughing at his own sarcasm.

"His name was David Bhaer," I responded. "Do you want to lose Beth the way I lost David?"

"No."

"Then make an effort," I pleaded. "You're not an island. What you do affects me, Beth, and our parents. We all love you and we couldn't go on if you give up. None of us could live through another loss. We need you!" I said, my face showing the strain. Daniel's shoulders began to shake and he cried out in frustration.

"Quentin was my twin, my other half," he exclaimed. "I was his protector. I watched his back. But I couldn't save him. I knew he wasn't feeling well. He told me about the stomach pain and the nausea. I thought it was a virus and told him to take something for the nausea and returned to my celebrating. All I was thinking of was Beth and me."

Stroking my brother's face, I said, "It's not your fault. How could you be expected to diagnose Quentin? You're not a doctor! What I don't understand," I said, "is why he didn't tell us how sick he was."

"You know Quentin. He never wanted to make a fuss. He didn't want to interfere with our celebration. remember, when he broke his collar bone and kept playing football?"

"Yes, I remember," I said.

Suddenly, Daniel was in my arms, letting go of the pain he had tried so hard to suppress. I knew it wouldn't be easy, but he would survive and his sorrow would lessen with time. I also knew things would never be the same. There would be a hole in Daniel's heart that even Beth couldn't fill.

After graduation, Daniel and Beth were married in the Chapel at Trinity Church. At the reception afterwards, Daniel raised his glass in a toast and said, "To my brother who is no longer with us physically but who is still in our hearts."

Daniel wasn't the only one who needed support after Quentin's death. There was Laurie, who had loved my brother and had hoped to marry him after graduation. I made a point of meeting her for lunch once a week and including Laurie in all family gatherings. Her reaction to Quentin's death reminded me of Ray after Lisa's accident. An outwardly friendly girl, Laurie changed overnight into a reserved, introspective stranger. What I didn't know at the time was that she was writing a short story, which would be published in a local magazine a year after Quentin's death. It was about my brother and his short but remarkable life.

Laurie was the middle of three girls. Her parents were both school teachers. Her mother taught tenth-grade English, her daddy general science and chemistry. Wally and Denise Cronister met while practice teaching in Corinth, Mississippi. Shortly after college graduation, they married and moved to Lancaster. Like Beth's family, Laurie's family was close-knit and full of fun. She, the most outgoing of the sisters, participated in every extra-curricular activity available to the active teenager. She was on the debate team, the drill team, the swimming team, and was editor of the school paper. It was simply a matter of time before she caught Quentin's eye. The two, so similar in temperament and outlook, seemed to mesh.

By her senior year at Belhaven College, Laurie, a dark-haired beauty who could stop traffic with her looks, decided on a career in journalism. Quentin, believing his girlfriend to be a talented writer, encouraged her ambitions. He agreed to attend a law school where Laurie could pursue graduate studies in journalism. Those plans came to an abrupt end with Quentin's death. So determined and focused before, she seemed to lose her way, not wanting to commit to anything, not even graduate school. During one of our weekly lunches, I encouraged Laurie to start a journal and to record her feelings in it. As I took the first bite of my grilled salmon, I broached the subject of the journal.

"Laurie, you can't keep it all in. Believe me, I know from experience that you need to share your feelings."

"I can't share, Katie, it's too painful."

I reached for the water in front of me and said, "Then write it down, honey. You have to let it out or it will drive you crazy."

"Maybe you're right. I think I could do that," said Laurie, sounding more positive than she had in quite awhile.

By our next luncheon, I could see a marked difference in her. Laurie, for the first time in months, was animated and talkative. We talked about Quentin and their past together, but we also talked of the future, Laurie's future.

"Well, I've decided it's time," said Laurie, smiling broadly.

"Time for what?" I questioned.

"To enroll in graduate school at Ole Miss."

"Laurie, I'm so happy for you!" I said, as I reached across the table to hug her.

"I'll miss our weekly lunches," she said.

"But you'll be back for holidays and it's only for a year," I said.

A year later, Laurie surprised me and my family with a wonderful gift that only she could give. She wrote about Quentin, his wonderful life and the positive effect that his life had on others. Laurie's article was moving and insightful. It appeared in a local magazine, but later that same article received national recognition. Laurie's older sister, a talented artist, presented us with a portrait of Quentin.

Laurie's gift provided my family with a lovely memory of my brother that we both cherished and needed. She eventually moved to New York and launched a successful career in television. The two of us remained close. The highlight of my year is my annual visit to New York during the last week in October. It's the week I spend with Laurie.

Chapter Twenty Seven
JANUARY 28, 1983

Mary Anne called David to tell him about Quentin. My sister didn't stop with the news of his death. Mary Anne told David that Quentin was his half brother. They met at Angie's for lunch. My sister told David how I found Mama's letters and the reason I broke off the affair. David went through the gamut of emotions. At first there was disbelief; finally anger and shock took over. He suddenly jumped to his feet, slammed money down on the table, and practically ran out of the restaurant. At least that's the way Mary Anne related it to Mama; Mama, in turn, told me. I wanted to kill Mary Anne, but Mama said my sister was just trying to help in her nosey, in-your-face way.

Two weeks after the funeral, I got a call from David requesting a meeting.

We met for drinks at a local bar located several blocks from the house I shared with Jeffery. Like most drinking establishments, Brady's was dimly lit. Nestled against the four walls were wooden booths. The bartender mixed his drinks at a circular bar located in the center of the room. His specialties included Black Russians and Brandy Alexanders. The ginger-colored walls were covered with pictures of antique cars and scenes of Jackson at the turn of the century. Brady's was a two-story building with the bar on the second floor and a deli serving soup and sandwiches on the first floor. The two floors were connected by a spiral staircase. I arrived half an hour before David and found a booth in the corner and ordered a gin and tonic. The juke box was playing "That's Amore." The minute I saw his face my heart began to pound. His eyes never left mine. They seemed to be searching for an answer, answers.

"Why didn't you tell me?" he asked.

"I didn't want to hurt you. I knew how much you loved your father. I figured it was something you couldn't get over," I explained.

"But I could get over loving you?" David asked.

"I figured the loss of me was easier than damaging your father's memory."

David's eyes clouded over. He leaned forward and took both my hands in his.

"Katie, I love you and I understand, but it's a lot to take in. I need time to think."

"Okay," I said, resigned to the loss of him. It's not like it was the first time I lost David.

Weeks passed, then months, and suddenly the year was gone and it was January again. David had left Mississippi and his job flying for Delta eight months before. He had taken a job with American Airlines and was living in Dallas. So I didn't expect to see him in the "Greasy Fingers," a local restaurant that specialized in fried shrimp and homemade comeback dressing.

The idea of attending a collegiate basketball tournament was not that enticing, but it was an opportunity to get out of the house and socialize with others. It had been a while since Jeffery and I had gotten together with his co-workers. We were to meet six other couples at the "Greasy Fingers" and then go to the coliseum to watch Ole Miss play Memphis State. Thanks to Jeffery's procrastination, we were late and the restaurant was overflowing with local fans of the competing teams.

Due to the wall-to-wall people in the tiny restaurant, I didn't notice David until halfway through the second serving of catfish and hushpuppies. The fact that he was only ten feet away from me started my pulse to racing. I debated whether I should go over and speak to David or let it go. He was sitting with his brother Phil and several cousins. The moment he saw me, David rose from the crowded table and met me halfway. I impulsively hugged him and exclaimed how good it was to see him. David saw through my little masquerade, looked deeply into my eyes and asked if I was okay. I lied and said "Yes, I'm okay."

"Are you sure, Katie?"

"Yes."

"Well, then I'm glad. But I can't help but wish you were free from Jeffery and totally mine."

I stared stupidly at him trying to think of something to say, but the words wouldn't come.

David continued. "I've had plenty of time to think and I realize I was a fool. Nothing matters but you and me."

"What about my mother and your father?" I asked.

"I'll never be a fan of your mother, but there's Daniel. I want to get to know him," said David.

I looked away and said, "I can't go through this again."

David continued to gaze at me, never saying a word or taking his eyes from my face. Finally, he leaned over and kissed me softly on the cheek, turned, and walked away. I stood there in the middle of the floor a full minute too shaken to move. Only Jeffery's voice calling me back to the table released me from my paralysis.

Later, at the tournament, I spotted him again. David was crossing the center edge of the basketball court, in order to speak to some friends from the rival team. I watched his lean, graceful figure until my heart began to pound so hard that I thought it would jump out of my chest. I tried to feign interest in the game, but my thoughts were full of him. The knowledge that he could still have such a devastating effect on me both amazed and irritated me.

Nothing had changed in all those years. It was like the first time I looked into his eyes and felt something that would never be altered or fade into mediocrity. The depth of my feelings were like some natural phenomena I didn't understand, but had faith in nonetheless. No matter how I tried to rationalize those feelings, I kept coming back to the undeniable. I loved David, and that was something that would never change. My life could alter dramatically, but loving him was my constant. I couldn't run from it, and in an instant I no longer wanted to. Whatever happened, I wanted to run toward David and all that entailed.

I hadn't smoked in years but later that night, I walked the floor and smoked cigarette after cigarette while Jeffery slept, undisturbed and oblivious, in an adjacent room. By the time daylight came, I had resolved to take action. I would plan carefully, locate a place to live, file for divorce, handle the financial aspects of a separation; none of it seemed too difficult when the future held the possibility of David. The conflict and the havoc dissipated, no longer a part of my psyche. I knew what I wanted, and with steely-eyed determination I was going after it. I picked up the phone and dialed the number. David answered on the first ring.

"I need to see you," I said.

"When and where?'

"Our neighborhood bar," I responded.

The moment I saw him, I raced into his arms. We talked for several hours and made our plans. We held hands, like teenagers. David's eyes never left mine. Not wanting it to end, we got a room at the Hilton and stayed the night. Jeffery was out of town on a one day trip to Greenville, but it didn't matter. All pretense was over as far as I was concerned. That night, David and I connected in a way that's hard to describe. I finally felt my wish had been granted. My body seemed to melt into his. We fell asleep, wrapped in each other's arms. The next day, I didn't want to leave, but David had a flight scheduled from Dallas to Newark, New Jersey. He promised to call once he had landed.

JANUARY 28, 1983

It was a drizzly January day - typical of winters in the Deep South, complete with a wet cold capable of chilling a person clean down to the bone. The dull overcast sky was reminiscent of the black and white films I watched every Saturday on the classics channel. Unlike those movies, this day would not end happily. It was almost two in the afternoon and I had still not heard from David. My stomach did flip-flops as I thought he had changed his mind once again.

The drizzle continued throughout the day, creating a mist that would not lift but lingered well past sundown. As night came, a purple-like haze ascended upon the atmosphere. Invariably, such a night evoked thoughts of London in my mind. I had yet to travel there, but my healthy imagination suggested that I was right. London looked like that during the winter months. Nights like this were my favorites. They held such possibilities, the romance and mystery of places unknown, people I had never met, and that old familiar ache for something I didn't know but had known once and had lost somewhere along the way.

Suddenly, I heard Jeffery's car in the driveway and braced for the confrontation that I knew was coming. Just as the front door opened, the telephone rang. At last I thought - David's calling. It wasn't David, it was my mother, her voice barely audible.

"Mama, what on earth? Is Daddy okay?"

"Yes, Katherine, your daddy's fine," she said almost choking on the words.

"Then what's going on?" I asked.

"I'm sorry, honey. David's plane went down; it's on the news."

Shaking like a leaf, I asked, "How badly was he hurt?"

"Baby, he's dead," responded Mama. "His plane went down in the Hudson River - engine failure, they think. Most of the passengers survived, but the pilots, both of them, were killed instantly."

"Mama, I've got to go, I'll call you back."

In a trance-like state, I went into the den and turned on the television set. There on the screen was the wreckage of the plane, debris floating in the water. Suddenly, everything went black. The next thing I knew, Jeffery was standing over me with a wet cloth.

TWO WEEKS LATER

I poured myself another glass of wine and replayed the song on the stereo for the tenth time. It was as if I were trying to absorb the words, memorize them for all time. The words told my life story - my anthem to a lost love and all the lost chances that died with David. The words to the Ray Charles song "I Can't Stop Loving You" physically hurt.

I felt my girlhood slipping away, realizing nothing would ever be the same. The sweet excitement, the joy of being near him, died in that crash. I would never again love without reserve, as unconditionally or as innocently as I had with David. Now there were no immediate decisions to be made, no confrontations. Life had relieved me of that responsibility.

Chapter Twenty Eight
JANUARY 28, 2000

It's been sixteen years since Katherine lost David. I grieved right along with her; not only for the death of her one true love, but for all the wasted time, all the mistakes that kept them apart so many years. The only good thing to come out of all the tragedies we endured was it brought us closer together as a family. Tom and I continued to grow as a couple, and it was I that supported Tom during Quentin's death.

When Dr. Pierce pronounced our son dead, my husband literally went to his knees and began sobbing like a baby. Between Daniel and myself, I managed to pick Tom up and practically carry him to the car. Once we got home, I held my husband in my arms for hours while he wept uncontrollably. During the wake and funeral afterwards, I never left Tom's side. When it was all over, he thanked me for not leaving him alone.

Later, Katherine and I were in Quentin's room sorting out his clothes, trying to decide what Daniel wanted to keep for himself and what we would give to charity, when Tom peeped around the corner and said, "Pat, can I speak to you for a minute?"

"Sure," I said, putting down a plaid shirt Quentin had recently worn. "What is it?"

"Baby, I want to thank you for supporting me through all of this," said Tom, with his voice cracking.

I rushed to him and put my arms around his waist and said, "You did the same thing for me through all of Mary Anne's troubles, remember?"

"Yes, I remember. What are we going to do without him, Pat?"

"As you told me before, we have to go on because we have other children who need us. Daniel needs you now more than ever."

He shook his head and hugged me.

As things turned out, we all helped each other. Mary Anne helped Tom stay sober, despite the gut-wrenching grief of losing another child. And Tom, along with Katherine, helped Daniel deal with the loss of his twin brother. I tried to be there for all of them. Sometimes I felt I was stretching myself too thin, but it kept me from losing it completely. I did my grieving alone. Once a week, I went to the graveyard with fresh flowers and sat by my son's grave and talked for an hour. Each week I told him another story about his babyhood, his childhood and his adolescence, and why those stories made me grateful he had been a part of my life.

A few years passed and my ritual became more extended. Once I had knelt and prayed at my son's grave, I would pick myself up and go to another section of the cemetery and lay flowers on the graves of Frederick and David. One day, I ran into Katherine who was placing her own flowers at the base of David's headstone. She looked up and smiled when she saw me coming, laden with roses.

"Fancy meeting you here," she said, laughing.

"It's ironic, isn't it?" I said, placing my arm around her shoulder.

"Yes, I guess it is," she said, looking down at their graves. "You never forgot them and neither have I."

"Katherine, I wish things had been different."

"I know, Mama. I know."

I placed flowers on both graves, and we left the cemetery hand in hand.

I never told Tom the truth about the twins. After all, he was their father. He raised them, loved them, and buried one of them. So it wasn't a lie when I called Tom their father.

As the years passed, I hoped that my daughter would make a new life for herself and find someone like David. But I didn't press the point. It was her life, and she didn't need me telling her what to do. But that didn't stop Mary Anne who tried to fix everything and everyone who needed fixing, according to her. It was her new hobby. Shopping was still fun, but no longer held the same thrills for her. After Katherine begged me "to do something with Mary Anne", as she put it, I called my daughter and asked her to take me shoe shopping. As we tried on summer sandals, I confronted Mary Anne about her "fix-it" behavior.

"Dear, we need to talk about Katherine…"

"What about Katherine, what's wrong now?" interrupted Mary Anne.

"Nothing's wrong. You need to cool it and let Katherine run her own life. You're driving her crazy!"

"Mama, I was just trying to help. She needs a man in her life, the right kind of man."

As I looked at handbags that might match the sandals I had picked out, I said. "That's for Katherine to decide. Mary Anne, have you ever thought about directing your energy into helping others in rehab, maybe sponsoring someone? You know that sort of thing!"

"And, get off Katherine's back?" she asked.

My daughter laughed and agreed to direct her need to get involved in other people's lives elsewhere.

As the years rolled by, I realized how lucky I was despite everything I had been through. That realization hit me at the most unusual times; in the middle of a family cookout, watching a college football game, or Tom's favorite game show on TV.

We were watching "Who Wants To Be A Millionaire", when that realization hit me right between the eyes. I was married to a man I truly loved, and I loved him more than the boy who died in the war, more than Frederick. Over the years, my husband had turned into the love of my life. Despite all the pain we had inflicted on one another, the betrayals, the fights, and the insults – despite all that, we grew together and fell in love with each other.

I looked at my husband and smiled. He was sitting in his favorite chair and shouting the answers before the contestants said a word. I reached out and grabbed his hand and said, "You know I love you, don't you?"

He smiled back at me, and said, "Yes, dear, and I love you, too. Now let me watch my show."

I had been wrong all those years ago when my children were growing up. My marriage was not a mistake.

It had been years since I had seen Betsy. She had come to spend the week with me. I had cleaned the house from top to bottom and planned a full schedule of fun things to do. I wanted everything to be perfect. I wondered whether Betsy had changed much, and whether she would think I had changed a lot.

As I pulled up to the drive-through at Evers International, I saw her standing by the curb. She looked the same. I stopped, jumped out of the car, and gave my friend a big hug. We talked incessantly for the next four hours. We paused just long enough for Betsy to unpack.

My home was located in the historic Belhaven District of Jackson. I had moved there after my divorce from Jeffery. It was quite a change from that mammoth Eastover mansion I lived in previously. My former husband had insisted on a large house with five bedrooms, a large library, den, breakfast room, restaurant-style kitchen as well as sunken bathtubs and a spiral staircase. I used to joke that we needed the theme from Tara installed instead of a regular doorbell chime. Jeffery, of course, didn't find my witty remark amusing. After the divorce, I found a home in Belhaven near the first home I had shared with Jeffery. I loved the area. Each house had its own unique style, unlike that cookie cutter look of most modern subdivisions. Belhaven had the aura of a small town nestled in the heart of metro Jackson. My home had three bedrooms and three baths. I had an old-fashioned kitchen with wooden floors and a window overlooking my tree-lined backyard. I didn't have a formal living room, but I did have a large and very comfortable den with a brick fireplace and a sliding glass door that led to a patio where I cooked out with my neighbors and family. My home had a comfy Early-American motif with lots of copper and pewter and scenes of ships on the open sea. It was so different from my former home, with its heavy dark furniture and opulent chandeliers in almost every room. After I gave Betsy the "grand tour," we headed for my favorite room. Halfway down the hall, she asked about my family.

"How are your parents?"

"Okay. Well, better than okay. After years of fighting, Mama and Daddy actually enjoy each other's company."

"How did that happen?" asked Betsy, obviously intrigued by my response.

"I'll have to think about that one for a minute," I said. "Good question though."

As we entered the den, I gave Betsy my answer. "Mama and Daddy survived a lot together - the death of two children and Mary Anne's drug problem. I think it made them closer," I explained. "They had to depend on each other to get through it all. And Daddy's in recovery. He actually goes to meetings with Mary Anne."

"You're kidding. That's amazing," exclaimed Betsy.

"Well, Daddy couldn't say no. Mary Anne has turned into a force to be reckoned with," I laughed. "Betsy, you wouldn't believe it! My sister is a national spokesperson on addiction and a successful businesswoman to boot."

"I still can't believe your sister, of all people, opened her own decorating firm. And she never remarried?" questioned Betsy.

"No," I responded. "Terry changed Mary Anne in ways even I don't understand. He was her great love and it nearly destroyed her. My sister closed the book on that part of her life. But she's a survivor and what she experienced made her realize she could take control and be whatever she wanted to be."

I headed toward the wet-bar looking for the wine glasses I had purchased from Pier 1. After locating the glasses, I told Betsy that Daniel had opened his own gallery in the Fondren area and that Beth had just given birth to their fourth child - a boy after three girls.

I poured two glasses of wine and we nestled into some over-stuffed chairs in the den. As I leaned back in my chair, I took a sip of wine and prepared myself for the question.

"Is there anyone special?"

"No," I said. "Not enough time."

Jeffery and I divorced four years after David's death. I went back to school and eventually got my graduate degree. With monthly support from Jeffery and the money I make as a college professor, I was able to feed and clothe myself and my son, Quentin. Teaching and raising Quentin have left little time for men. Despite that fact, there had been a few half-hearted attempts at romance, but nothing that led to anything serious.

I told Betsy I had ended up teaching everything we had lived through in the sixties. As I grew older, I realized how little I understood about those times. The world around me broke apart and reshaped itself. The Vietnam War and Civil Rights left their mark, but nothing mattered as much as a boy named David. I often wondered how much I missed with that single-minded focus. I also wondered if anyone in my white, middle-class existence could really understand the significance of the Civil Rights Movement or a war that politicians called a conflict.

"It's funny," I said as I poured a second glass of wine for the two of us. "All this history was happening around us and we were on the edge of it, never really in the thick of it."

"But it changed us nonetheless," commented Betsy.

"True, but I wish I had been in the middle of things, shaking things up. Remember what I was like in high school?"

"Yes," laughed my friend. "You were very outspoken. You and your mother used to have some major fights over your views. If I remember correctly," she chuckled, "some were violent."

"Yes, they were. But that's all I did – mouth off! Even when Ray died, I did nothing. I managed to live through the sixties without ever participating in one anti-war demonstration. Pretty pathetic!"

"I think you had more influence than you think. Look at the twins," Betsy pointed out.

"Yes, but there's so much I didn't do. My focus was on other things."

"Yes, I know."

"And, then there was my marriage to Jeffery. My refusal to leave him cost me a wonderful friendship. That's why I tell my students not to be afraid to act, to get out there and stir things up."

"What finally made you leave the bastard?"

"I found out about his uncle's connection with the Klan. It seems Uncle Billy had been involved in a number of violent incidents involving blacks and, of course, Jeffery thought Billy was wonderful."

"Sick."

"Yes, sick, and then there were all the lies that finally came out."

"What?"

"Jeffery's parents didn't die when he was eight years old. His father was a drunk who used to beat Jeffery, and his mother was the town whore who slept with every man above the age of eighteen."

"Oh, my God, I don't believe it," exclaimed Betsy, obviously shocked by what I had told her.

"Yes, and his parents didn't die until after he met me."

"You mean when y'all were at Belhaven?"

"Yes, it all came out four years after David's death. It must have been the hundredth time I asked him for a divorce. He finally agreed but not before telling me the sordid details of his pathetic life. Boy, am I glad to be rid of him!"

"Where is he now?"

"Still practicing corporate law, married a girl twenty years younger than him and dumb as a post."

Thankfully, Betsy's life with Herb and her four boys was a happy one. She told me that if anything happened to Herb, she would never remarry because she was sure she would never find anyone as wonderful as Herb. Betsy relayed that two of her sons taught school. Another had gone to law school, and the fourth boy, the baby, became a heart surgeon. She had ten grandchildren and a great grandchild on the way. It was obvious my friend was proud of her boys and devoted to her husband.

After updating me on her family, she asked, "How about you Katie, are you happy?"

"Yes, I think so."

"You think so. Aren't you sure?"

"Yes, I'm sure," I responded. "You know Quentin was a little miracle."

"I guess so at forty. I bet your parents were pleased that you named your son after your brother."

"Yes," I said, "and I think David would approve also."

"What does David have to do with it?" asked Betsy.

"We'll get to that later," I cautioned.

But Betsy wouldn't drop the subject.

"I'm surprised you still think about David. I thought you had forgotten him."

"I never forgot him."

"Katherine, do you really think you loved David? After all, you were only fourteen."

I wanted to point out the absurdity of that question, but I didn't. The fact that I had felt it made it real.

"You seem lost in thought," my friend observed.

"I'm thinking about how I should answer your question. The only answer I know is that it certainly felt real. He was the only man I've ever known who could make me feel shy and tongue tied, long after I reached adulthood. Funny thing is, I can still feel that heart-thumping excitement when I think of him. Yes, I loved him and I always will."

"But is that enough?" asked Betsy.

Suddenly the door opened, and there stood my son. His lean graceful form dominated the room. He had his father's broad shoulders and long tapered hands; and, of course, his father's brown eyes that had the same deepness and intensity, those same eyes that focused on you when you talked.

Betsy made the appropriate responses as I introduced my son, but the look on her face said it all. She knew. After she recovered from the shock, she asked, "Quentin, I understand you got your law degree. Are you going to practice with Jeffery -- I mean your father?"

"No, Miss Betsy. I want to fly commercially. I've applied with Delta, United, and American Airlines."

"Quentin just got his pilot's license," I interjected.

My son visited with us until his girlfriend called about their dinner date later that night. When Quentin left the room, Betsy asked the question she had been wanting to ask for over an hour.

"Does he know?"

"No," I said. "I haven't told him. I'm still not sure whether I should."

"But Katie, he has a right to know."

"But I don't know whether it would do more harm than good," I explained.

"Does Jeffery know?" asked Betsy.

"I think so. He certainly suspects."

"What about your family?"

"Yes, Mama and Mary Anne know. I'm not sure whether Daddy and Daniel know. They certainly don't know the whole story."

"Well, I can't imagine that everyone doesn't realize. All you have to do is look at Quentin and you know who his father is," exclaimed Betsy.

I laughed at her response and said with a smile, "And you asked if I still thought of David."

I hope you have enjoyed *Just Out of Reach!* You can find me on Twitter @BelindaSteven20 on Facebook at facebook.com/belinda.stevens.733 or on my blog at belindastevens.blogspot.com. As a special bonus, I've included the first two chapters of my next book "Justice Served," which will be released in early 2014.

JUSTICE SERVED

By: Belinda Stevens

CHAPTER ONE

They found him in the inner sanctum of his law office, deader than a doornail, with his severed forefinger shoved halfway down his throat. No one knew whether he died of shock resulting from the loss of blood or as a result of a heart attack brought on by sheer, unadulterated terror. But I knew, because I severed the finger and I caused his untimely, but well-deserved, death!

There was a gathering at Joe's Diner across from the courthouse. It's where the local attorneys and court clerks go for their morning coffee. They were all talking about the gruesome discovery. I sat at a table in the corner and eavesdropped on their comments. I almost laughed out loud at their "who done it" theories. If they only knew, I thought. Wouldn't they be surprised?

"Who found the body?"

"I think it was Sara Beth. They said you could hear her screams all the way in the parking lot!"

"Well, you know Sara Beth. She always was a screamer."

"That's not funny, Ralph."

"Oh, Susie, give me a break. Where's your sense of humor? You know Judge Edwards deserved exactly what he got."

Martin laughed. "I'm glad somebody finally found a good use for that finger of his."

Ralph chuckled. "Whoever killed the bastard should have stuck that finger where the sun don't shine."

Ralph and Susie were Public Defenders who had endured Judge Edwards' finger-wagging and general abuse for the last four years. Martin was the newly elected Circuit Clerk. He had defeated the Judge's brother-in-law, so there was no love lost between Martin Wilson and Judge Edwards. Bad blood had existed between the Edwards and Wilson families for several generations.

Martin's grandfather, a former prosecutor, hounded Judge Edwards' great-uncle out of office. Not only was Raymond Edwards forced to resign as County Court Judge, he ended up serving time for one hundred thousand dollars ($100,000.00) in kickbacks and other nefarious activities. It would seem the fickle finger of fate would point to Martin as a likely suspect. But Lancaster County's newly elected Circuit Clerk had an iron-clad alibi. He was being certified by the Secretary of State's Office and being sworn in by his best friend, Leslie Brooks, Mississippi's Senior Judge on the appellate court, at the time of the murder.

As I left the diner, I heard Susie say the local police were interviewing persons of interest, essentially everyone who was in the courthouse at the estimated time of death. The first to be interrogated was Sara Beth, the lady who found the Judge's body. Again, I laughed. They'd never figure this one out.

SARA BETH

I've been a court reporter for seventeen years. The last fifteen of those years I worked for Judge Edwards. The first day on the job, the Judge hit on me. I was single then but now I'm married with three children. The last time Judge Edwards came on to me was three days before his murder. Not only did the man look like a bulldog on a three day drunk, he was the nastiest, most chauvinistic son-of-a-bitch I've ever had the misfortune to know. I worked for him because I had a family to help feed and because I needed the years for state retirement, but there was no amount of money that could persuade me to sleep with that sleaze bag. I'm not sorry he's dead. I'm just sorry I'm the one who found his body.

As I entered the interrogation room, I began to shake. The sight of three detectives with various colored pictures of the severed finger and the Judge's battered body made me slightly nauseous.

"Please sit down, Ms. Spencer. Or is it Mrs.?"

"Detective Sparks, you know it's Mrs. and you've known that for at least eight years. That's how long you've been on the force, right?" I asked.

"Of course, Sara Beth, just a few questions, okay?"

"Okay."

"First of all, where were you between 8:00 A.M. and 10:00 A.M. this morning?"

"I was in the Clerk's Office having coffee with the girls until 9:15. After that, I went to the post office and then to the bank. I got back to the courthouse shortly before 10:00 A.M."

"Who did you see at the post office and at the bank?"

"Well, Miss Omega sold me stamps and Miss Nancy waited on me at the bank," I responded.

Next, Detective Taylor asked me about the discovery of the body. I told him the Judge's door was ajar but I had still knocked. When there was no answer, I entered and found the Judge lying face-up next to his desk. The first and only thing I noticed was the bloody finger sticking out of his mouth. I ran from the room screaming. Detective Sparks asked if I noticed anything else. I told him no; nothing out of place, just that grisly finger. After further questioning, I told Detective Banks if there had been anything out of place, I wouldn't have known; I was in too much of a hurry to get out of that room!

I knew the hideous discovery in my hometown would be on the nightly news and that my name would be mentioned. Tannersville is forty-five miles south of Jackson, the state capitol. It's located in a section of the state referred to as the Piney Woods area. This part of the state is mainly rural; where farmers meet at the local general store for morning coffee to discuss their neighbors, warts and all. Tannersville is one of the larger towns in the Piney Woods area with a population of fifteen thousand. It's a town still small enough for everyone to know everybody else's business, but the locals don't know everything about me. They considered me a local beauty queen that went to Ole Miss after graduating from high school. I majored in Journalism with a straight-A average. I mysteriously dropped out of college my senior year and only my family knows the reason why. I was the victim of a date rape. It wasn't until Jeff came along that I began to trust again. Two years after I starting working for Judge Edwards, I married Jeff.

My husband commutes every day to Jackson. He is the manager of a women's clothing store. Gentle and unceasingly patient, he always listens to my rants about the comments of the Judge and other local brain-dead males who seem obsessed with my full figure. What I didn't tell Detective Sparks is that if I had murdered Edwards, I would have castrated him – not cut off his finger!

CHAPTER II

After Sara Beth left the interrogation room, the detectives discussed her alibi and the general truthfulness of her statement. None of them knew that Edwards' killer was in an outer connecting room. No one saw me slip in and I remained quiet as a mouse as I took in every word they spoke. It was funny to listen to those keystone cops. They couldn't solve a simple robbery at high noon, much less a murder.

"What do you think?" asked Banks.

"I don't think she could have done it," responded Taylor. "First, she has an alibi that's easy to verify. Second, how could she subdue a man twice her height and weight and forcibly cut off his finger and then shove it halfway down his throat?"

"Maybe she drugged him," said Sparks, taking another sip of overcooked coffee that had been sitting out since 8:30 A.M. that morning.

"We don't have a pathology report, autopsy results or anything else – not even a murder weapon. So everything's only speculation at this point," stated Banks, pacing the floor.

"Well, I still say she's probably in the clear," said Taylor. The others agreed. At that point, they decided to take a break before questioning the District Attorney, Dan Scott. I hid in the bathroom while they filed past me into the hallway.

Dan Scott was Lancaster County's first black District Attorney. Most people gave him the benefit of the doubt, but not Judge Edwards. He goaded Dan every chance he got. When Edwards wasn't telling tasteless racist jokes, he was talking down to Dan as though the D.A. had a third grade education. Dan stood his ground. He never went over the line with Edwards but he didn't tolerate his insults either.

Judge Edwards was supporting Dan Scott's opponent in the upcoming August election for District Attorney. Dan had held the post of District Attorney for four years and was currently running for re-election. Everyone knew the guy running against Scott was an idiot who barely etched out a living with simple divorces, child custody disputes and preparation of wills, the kind that weren't contested. Charles Bass may have been a simpleton, but he was Judge Edwards' man, or lackey, so to speak. The fact that Edwards was so open in his support of Bass irked Dan Scott, but was it enough for murder?

DAN

As I entered the Interrogation Room and saw Sparks, Banks and Taylor sipping that awful courthouse coffee made by inmates four hours earlier, I thought about the first time I laid eyes on those men.

Shortly after my election, I went to the police station to introduce myself to the Chief. I was ushered into a room filled with suspicious faces, including the faces of Sparks, Banks and Taylor. The previous D.A. had alienated everyone with her impossible demands; her way of putting things off until the last minute, and her refusal to return phone calls or communicate with the police on active cases.

I did my best to assure everyone I didn't operate that way. It took a full year, but I gained most people's confidence, although Sparks still didn't like me. Detective Sparks didn't like anyone whose skin wasn't lily-white, and who wasn't male and protestant. Since I was black and Catholic, Sparks didn't trust me as far as he could throw me, which wasn't very far, especially since he was the Donut King of Lancaster County.

Sparks was twenty pounds overweight but considered himself a "ladies man". He boasted that he had three girlfriends in the three surrounding counties, and managed to see each girl at least every other day. He said he burned up the roads visiting his lady friends.

Naturally, Sparks was the first to question me about my whereabouts when Judge Edwards was murdered. Much to his dismay, I was interviewing witnesses in an upcoming case, with both of my assistants present during the interviews. God knows, I wasn't sorry Edwards was gone because he made my life a living hell, and the bastard ruled against me on everything. I couldn't prove it, but it was an open secret that Edwards would rule any way you wanted him to for the right fee. The Judge would give light sentences to repeat offenders if the money passing hands was substantial enough. People said at the end of the day, the length of a defendant's sentence depended solely on the amount of money in the Judge's wallet. No, I didn't kill the son-of-a-bitch, but I'm glad he's dead, and that's exactly what I told Sparks, Banks and Taylor!

AUTHOR BIO

Belinda J. Stevens was born in Yazoo City, Mississippi, the gateway to the Mississippi Delta, in 1948. She grew up in the turbulent sixties, and has a true appreciation for the difficulties experienced by Katherine in *Just Out of Reach,* which is Belinda's first novel. She is an attorney who currently practices law in Yazoo City and resides in Brandon, Mississippi with her dog, Humprey B.